BROOKLYN'S BRIDGE

by
Gary Guest

Words Matter Publishing
P.O. Box 531
Salem, Il 62881
www.wordsmatterpublishing.com

ISBN 13: 978-1-949809-38-1
ISBN 10: 1-949809-38-2

Library of Congress Catalog Card Number: 2019946672

DEDICATION

I'd like to thank my great-niece Brooke for inspiring me to finish this book. The idea for this story was in my head for a number of years and it was through the urging of Brooke that I sat down and completed it. I believe that motivating others in life will be one of her many talents.

I couldn't have done it without you Brooke. Thanks to a (GREAT) great-niece.

Uncle Gary

Chapter 1
THE BEGINNING

September 28, 1924. Today was the day. The captain of the passenger ship, Victoria, had told the passengers that when they awoke this morning, they would be in New York Harbor. German immigrants, Henry and Ella Borgman were among the thousand or so passengers that had left their homelands for a chance to live in America. Henry and Ella had hoped for several years that they could someday join Henry's cousin Andrew and call America home. With the political unrest in Germany, they decided now was the time.

The Borgmans, along with most of the other immigrants lined Victoria's railing as the morning sky began to lighten. They were all expecting to see the New York City skyline. What they saw was fog. The fog was so thick that the Victoria had dropped anchor and was afraid to move for fear of running aground. Minutes turned into a half hour. Then an hour. As the anxious moments ticked by, Henry's mind drifted back to his homeland and to the events that had helped them decide to leave Germany. Henry's father Otto, and Andrew's father John were brothers and worked together in a small lumber supply business that they owned. Henry and Andrew had no brothers or sisters, so the two of them grew up as if they were siblings. Life for these two Borgman families was better than the average German household of that time. The first struggles that Herman and Andrew would ever experience in their lives came in the form of World War I. Otto and John were not young enough to be front-line soldiers, so they were recruited to work in a factory that produced the gases that were used in chemical warfare. As the "war to end all wars," drug on, things got harder and harder on the German citizens.

In the winter of 1917, Andrew's mother died of pneumonia. Andrew stayed with Henry and his mom Leona while their fathers continued to work for the government. As World War I was drawing to a close, things were rough in the Borgman's home. There was no heat and food was in short supply. Leona always managed to get the boys some kind of meal, but she seldom looked out for her own nourishment. Just after the armistice was signed ending the war, Leona passed away. The cause of death was malnutrition. So now in the postwar days, the four Borgman men found themselves trying to build some facsimile of life. Otto and John tried to run their lumber store again, but none of the citizens had any money. Henry and Andrew began working for a man who worked on cars and trucks. The two boys were fast learners and absorbed most of what they were taught as they grew into fine young men. Tragedy reared its ugly head again in the boys' lives when in the summer of 1921 it became apparent that both their dads were sick and dying. In July of that year, both Otto and John succumbed to their illnesses. All the family and friends knew their deaths were a direct result of the chemicals they worked with during the war. However, the German government vehemently denied that the death of the Borgman brothers was related to the war. Henry and Andrew continued on the best they could and it was shortly after the passing of their fathers that Andrew began to talk of leaving Germany and starting a new life in America. Henry agreed, and the two cousins started planning for that to happen.

Then Henry had a snag rise up in his life. It was a good snag. He met a beautiful young lady named Ella, and after only a few get-togethers he was convinced that she could be more than a friend. Andrew was happy for his cousin, but his mind stayed focused on going to America. Henry and Ella's romance blossomed and in less than a year they were husband and wife. Ella was well aware of Henry and Andrew's plans to go to America but for her things were more difficult. Ella's parents and two sisters lived in a small berg not far from Berlin. While the Borgman cousins had little to hold them there, for Ella to be ready to leave Germany would take a little time. So eventually the cousins agreed that Andrew would go on to America and write back to Henry and Ella all that he discovered in this new land. In the spring of 1923, Henry and Ella saw Andrew off as he boarded the ocean liner that would carry him and his dreams to America.

A couple of months after leaving, Andrew sent his first letter back to his cousin. Andrew was fast falling in love with New York City. His letter told of a great chance at a new life and plenty of opportunities for the Borgman cousins in America. His subsequent letters told of his new employment and the fact that there was probably room for Henry to work at the same place. Andrew's letters fueled the fire that burned inside Henry and they helped to convince Ella that America was in her destiny. If Henry and Ella needed more help in deciding what to do, it was provided by Germany itself. It was less than five years after the end of World War I, but in the spring and summer of 1924, rumblings were being heard around the country about a new branch of political government that was dissatisfied with the current leaders and was working to overthrow the people now in power. Gossip in the countryside spoke of possible war returning to Germany. Ella needed no more convincing. They said their goodbyes, got their paperwork in order and climbed aboard the Victoria.

Like that, the sounds of someone yelling snapped Henry out of his reminiscing and brought him back to the present.

"There it is! I see it!" The fellow passengers strained their eyes in the direction of the pointing fingers. With a slight breeze, the fog thinned enough to reveal the object of their intent. The Statue of Liberty. Lady Liberty stood ready to welcome another boatload of dreamers into this land of freedom known as the melting pot. Cheers and tears were abundant on the deck of the Victoria. Regardless of where each immigrant had called home, in a short while they could all share the title of American.

Henry and Ella were like many of the other passengers in that they had brought very few possessions with them. They had packed some pictures, and some special mementos but whatever else they had owned back in Germany had been sold or given to family or friends. They debarked from the boat with their few bags and then waited in the line on Ellis Island to sign their names into history. When it was their turn at a check-in table, they presented their credentials and signed the register. With a big smile and in his best English Henry proudly told the officer "Now we are Americans!"

The unimpressed agent glumly looked up and replied, "Good for you pal. Next."

Henry and Ella slowly made their way off the peer and into the crowded streets lined with the newcomers as well as the vendors and hawkers looking to make a quick buck. They held tight their bags as they searched for Henry's cousin Andrew who had promised to meet them when they arrived. Andrew stood on a set of stairs as he perused the masses in hopes of finding the Borgmans. Halfway up the street, Henry heard Andrew's voice. "Henry. Ella. Over here!" They spied Andrew waving to them. They fought through the crowd and soon joined up with Andrew. Handshakes, hugs and welcomes were enthusiastically exchanged. Andrew said, "Let's get out of this crowd." They followed Andrew for a couple of blocks until they reach the parking lot where Andrew had parked his car. Soon the trio was away from the harbor crowd and on their way to the little house that Andrew had rented for them. Henry and Ella's house was only a block away from Andrew's home and only a half mile from the garage where Andrew worked and where Henry planned to. The little white-sided house held only about nine hundred square feet of living area, but to Henry and Ella, it looked perfect.

Andrew pulled a key out of his pocket and handed it to Henry. "Go open the door to your first American home." Henry's smile couldn't have been any bigger as the door swung open. Not just the door to their house, but also the door of opportunity in the land of the free. Henry and Ella…welcome Home.

Chapter 2
ADDITION TO THE FAMILY

For the rest of that week, Henry and Ella went about the business of becoming familiar with their neighborhood and stocking their home with some necessities. On Monday morning Henry kissed Ella goodbye and joined Andrew in the half-mile walk to work. Andrew introduced Henry to his boss, Dave Elders. Dave shook Henry's hand, then said, "Andrew says that you're a good engine mechanic and that you're looking for a job."

Henry replied, "Well, he's right in that I am looking for work and I hope he's right when he says I'm a good mechanic."

"Henry, if you're anything like Andrew, I think you'll work out just fine. Of course I can't pay you full wages until I see some of your work. You understand?"

Henry told Dave that was fine and he graciously

appreciated the opportunity to prove himself. "Sounds great," said Dave. "Andrew can show you around the shop a little bit then maybe you two can try to figure out why that Ford over there doesn't run." Dave pointed to the old car in the far bay. In just a few minutes the two cousins were elbow-deep under the hood of the Ford. For Henry and Andrew, it seemed like old times. Back in Germany, the Borgman cousins had a good reputation for keeping the cars they worked on in good running condition. Andrew was probably the better of the two Borgman cousins when it came to working on the insides of a motor, but Henry seemed to have a special knack when it came to setting carburetors or the spark. Together they made a good team whenever they worked on a vehicle. Later on that afternoon, Dave was in his office when he heard the Ford come to life. After a few minutes of fine tuning, the car ran as good as it did when it was new. Henry happened to glance toward the office door and saw Dave smiling. Henry grinned back and gave his new boss a little wave. Henry's employment was off to a good start.

Dave Elders proved to be a wonderful boss, and in a short time, he would also become a good friend. He continually passed along his knowledge of autos to the Borgman cousins. This was a big help, especially in regards to the newer cars that were being produced every year.

In the next few months, Henry really settled into his city life. He liked his boss and coworkers, and he was quickly falling in love with New York City. Ella was equally happy with their new life. Henry and Ella had followed Andrew's lead in coming to America, and they also followed him to the nearby Lutheran Church. Trinity Lutheran Church was only two blocks from their home, and the people there seemed very friendly as they welcomed the Borgmans into the congregation. It took a lot of faith for the couple to make their journey across the ocean and as they traveled through their lives, their faith would be tested many more times.

One morning as Henry was about to leave for work, Ella informed Henry that she hadn't been feeling very well and so she was going to go see a doctor. Henry asked if he should stay home from work and go with her. She smiled and replied that it wasn't that bad and she could see the doctor on her own. Henry kissed her and headed to work. Ella didn't tell Henry that she already had a suspicion as to what was making her stomach queasy. The doctor confirmed her diagnosis…. Ella was pregnant. Henry and Ella were always planning for a family, but during the first four years of their marriage, they were uncertain if they wanted to have children in the political unrest of Germany. Now the time was right. Ella was as happy as she could be that afternoon while she tried to think of a special way to tell Henry. Ella prepared one of Henry's favorite meals. When Henry came home from work, the first thing he did was ask Ella how she was feeling. She smiled and told him she was feeling much better now. She told him to wash up and come to the dinner table. Henry sat down at the table and prepared to fill his plate when he realized that there were three place settings on the table. He quizzically looked at Ella and asked, "Are we having company?"

Ella coyly smiled and replied, "No. I'm just getting in the practice of setting another place for our family."

It took Henry a few more seconds for the male mind to get the hint, then wide-eyed he looked at Ella and asked, "You're pregnant?" Ella was beaming as she nodded yes. Henry leapt from his chair, knocking it over as he raced around the table to embrace his wife. Their tears intermingled on each other's cheeks as they kissed and hugged in celebration. Henry looked up and said, "Thank You Lord! Thank You!" They spent a good part of the rest of the evening holding onto one another as their minds raced with the joy of starting a family.

Henry and Ella were quick to share their good news with Andrew, Dave and a host of new friends they had made through work and church. Time went by fast as Henry and Ella prepared for the day that their family would grow. A couple of months before the baby was to arrive, Henry told Ella that Dave had found them a good deal on a used car. It needed a little work, but Henry could fix it up on his own time. Having a means of transportation would allow the Borgmans to further explore the city and the lands around it. Ella agreed that having their own car would be nice. Henry and Andrew began staying an hour or so after work to fix up Henry's car. By the following Saturday, they had the car out on the road for a test run. The car ran smoothly and Henry was all smiles when he pulled up in front of the house to show Ella. Almost every week-end Henry and Ella would find time to go for a drive somewhere. They loved finding new places to see and visit, both in the city and outside of it and it was on one of their trips that Ella told Henry that while she loved the house they lived in, she hoped that someday as their family grew, they could buy their own house in the country. Henry agreed that that would be nice, but they would have to save up for a few years before that could happen.

When Ella's due date was about a month away, the ladies at the Trinity Lutheran Church threw her a baby shower. The Borgmans received many nice gifts, but the nicest of all was a handcrafted cradle made by one of the men of the church. Henry and Ella were sure they couldn't be more blessed.

On a beautiful October Sunday afternoon, about two weeks before the baby was scheduled to arrive, Henry asked Ella if she would like to go for a drive and possibly have a picnic in a park somewhere. Ella replied that it sounded wonderful, but she added, "Let's not get too far away from the hospital. Just in case." As the two of them sat on a blanket in the park, the conversation turned to a familiar subject. What to name the baby. They threw out boys and girls names left and right, but nothing seemed quite right. Henry and Ella agreed on one point…. They wanted their child to have an American name. Naming the baby after one of the family back in Germany was out of the question. As far as deciding on a name, nothing was settled, and after a little lunch, Henry and Ella packed up and headed for home. Their route home would take them back across the Brooklyn Bridge. To them, this bridge was an engineering masterpiece, and it seemed to embody the "can-do" attitude that they loved here in America. They marveled at the structure any time they crossed it.

As they were crossing the bridge, they were still throwing out baby names when Henry suddenly noticed the cars in front of them coming to an immediate halt. Henry stopped the car as he wondered what was going on. In front of him a ways he could see drivers getting out of their cars. Henry told Ella he was going to walk up and see if he could find out what was going on. After walking past twenty cars are so, Henry could see the problem. A produce truck had collided with a car, overturning the truck and scattering its load. The entire bridge was blocked. Henry was a little annoyed but figured they could get the mess straightened out soon, so he proceeded back to his car. He looked in through the driver's window as he prepared to tell Ella the news. What he saw caused his words to freeze on his lips. Ella had a terribly frightened look on her face as she faced Henry. Tears were flowing down her cheeks as she said, "Henry. My water just broke! I'm going to have the baby!" Henry was by nature a calm person, but all rationale left him as he tried to comprehend what to do.

"Are you sure you're all right?" he asked Ella for the third time.

Fighting through a contraction pain, Ella yelled, "Yes, I'm fine! Please find some help!"

Henry ran circles around his car as he yelled at the top of his lungs, "My wife is having a baby! Can somebody please help?" Henry's frantic cries caused drivers around him to pass the word along. An elderly gentleman and a middle-aged woman emerged from a car about fifty yards away. He was a doctor, and the lady was his nurse. They were returning from a house call when they had become entangled in the traffic jam. Was it fate? Or was it divine intervention that put the doctor and nurse on the bridge at this precise time. No one knows for sure, but the Borgman's guardian angel was on the job. The doctor grabbed his bag from the back seat, and the pair made their way to the Borgman's car.

Henry was still yelling when the doctor placed his hand on Henry's shoulder. "My name is Dr. James. This is Nurse Watson. Can we be of any help?"

"Oh thank God," cried Henry. "My wife is having a baby. I don't know what to do!"

Henry led the doctor to Ella's car door. After opening the door, the doctor smiled at Ella and said, "Don't worry young lady. You're going to be just fine. What's your name?"

Between pains, Ella replied, "My name is Ella, but my baby's not due for two weeks!"

"Well," answered Dr. James, "babies usually arrive whenever they want to. I suspect your baby just wanted an audience. Let's try to get you lying down in the backseat." They maneuvered Ella to the backseat. Henry opened the back door on the driver's side and knelt next to Ella's head. He placed her hand in his and told her that he loved her. Dr. James looked around at the gathering crowd and announced, "Please people. Give us a little room to work. We will let you know when this 'new' New Yorker gets here."

Even though this was Ella's first baby, things happened pretty fast. Less than a half hour passed before the cries of a healthy baby rang out to the crowd. The cries of the baby were drowned out by a roar of celebration from the folks gathered around. Dr. James motioned for Henry to come around to the passenger side of the car. Strangers were slapping Henry on the back as he passed behind his car. As Dr. James stood up, he cradled the towel-wrapped baby in his arms. He passed the baby to Henry and said, "Here Dad, he's asking for you. Congratulations, you have a son!" Another roar went up from the surrounding crowd. Shouts of congratulations could be heard up and down the bridge.

When the noise had died down, one New Yorker yelled to Henry, "Hey buddy. What are you going to name him—Brooklyn?" That question was followed by a round of laughter from the crowd. That impromptu question now had the name of Brooklyn resonating around inside of Henry's head. Henry looked in the car at his wife who was smiling back at him. She had heard the question as well. Without saying a word, she nodded her approval to Henry.

Henry turned to face in the general direction of the inquiry. Holding the baby up he replied, "Yeah, I think we will! Say hello to Brooklyn!"

Another roar went up. More congratulations were

hailed in Henry's direction as the crowd made their way back to their cars. Dr. James told Henry he needed to take Ella and Brooklyn to the hospital to get checked out. "My nurse can ride with you and hold the baby. I'll meet you there." Henry made Ella as comfortable as possible, then climbed behind the steering wheel next to nurse Watson holding Brooklyn. Cars were starting to get past the accident site, and in five minutes Henry was on the road heading for the hospital. Henry gave the nurses at the hospital all the information while Ella and Brooklyn were taken in to be examined and admitted. When the paperwork was done, Henry collapsed into one of the waiting room chairs. Total exhaustion was hitting him like a freight train. He silently offered up his prayers of thanksgiving to the good Lord. Ten minutes or so had passed when Henry heard footsteps approaching his chair. He raised his head out of his folded hands to see the smiling faces of Doc James and Nurse Watson. His legs felt like jelly as he stood to embrace the two angels he felt God had provided. Doc James told Henry, "I just checked with the doctors and mother and baby are in perfect health. But I'm a little worried about the father though." Doc James broke into a big laugh as he asked, "Are you going to be all right?"

Henry replied, "There's not a thing in this world that could make me feel better than I do right now. How can I ever thank you?"

Doc replied, "Oh, I suppose you could stop by my office sometime and give me a little bit for our time. But it's no rush."

Henry assured him that he would pay him for everything he and Nurse Watson had done. Henry again shook their hands then the doctor and nurse headed for the parking lot. Just before they reached the exit doors, Henry called out to them, "Hey Doc. I forgot to tell you. His middle name is going to be James. It's Brooklyn James Borgman."

Dr. James broke into a big smile. "In that case, I'm cutting my fee in half." They all laughed. The doctor and nurse headed for their car. Henry plopped back down in the chair waiting to be told that he could see his family. Henry's thoughts swirled as he tried to soak in all that it happened in the past few hours. When they had left home sightseeing was really all that was on his mind. And now he was a father. It's not that he hadn't thought about it before, but as he sat in this hospital waiting room, his heart raced with the excitement and joy of having a son to the fear of all the responsibilities that lay ahead of him.

With no one around him to hear, he refolded his hands and cast his eyes upward and spoke, "Please guide me and help me make wise decisions." He then closed his eyes and bowed his head and waited.

The staff at the hospital all marveled at the story of Brooklyn's arrival and to how he had acquired his name. Just before being discharged from the hospital, one of the doctors asked, "With the name of Brooklyn, won't people think your baby is a girl?"

"Yah," Henry replied. "We kind of thought of that. His official name is still going to be Brooklyn, with the bridge and all. But we plan on calling him Brooks."

Henry and Ella thanked all the folks at the hospital then pointed the nose of their car towards home.

A few weeks after his arrival, Brooks was christened at the church. Andrew was beaming as he held his godson for the ceremony. Dr. James was there for the services as well, and the minister informed the congregation the role the doctor played in Brooks's birth. He said, "The good Lord does indeed provide for the needs of his people. With the manner in which Brooks arrived. I predict the Lord will always be there. Anytime Brooks needs it." No one knew then how prophetic that would prove to be. After the service, a small celebration was held at the Borgman house. Things were wonderful in Henry and Ella's world.

Chapter 3
TOUGH TIMES

The events of Brooks's younger years could pretty well be described as normal. There were birthdays, Christmases, Easter's, Fourth of July's and such. And through these early years, Brooks proved to be a very bright and inquisitive child.

A few years after Brooks was born the Borgmans did receive some very disappointing news. Henry and Ella had been trying for a while to conceive another child. Nothing seemed to be happening. So Ella made an appointment and went to see her doctor. After some tests, the doctors doubted that Ella would ever get pregnant again. While Henry and Ella had truly wished to have a larger family, they were always incredibly grateful for the special son that they had. Brooks was a constant source of joy for this young New York family.

Henry stayed busy at the garage. Ella was equally busy raising Brooks, keeping house, as well as helping teach Sunday school. Henry made a decent salary at the garage, but most of the income was eaten up in monthly bills. They had no extra money to speak of so it was that they did not pay a lot of attention to the rumblings of an impending economic crisis. When the stock market crashed, and the depression began, Henry and Ella didn't realize the magnitude effect this event would have on all of America. The brokers, investors and bankers were some of the first people to panic. The money that the Borgmans were able to save from Henry salary was kept in a box at their home. So with no savings account or stock market holdings, they failed to understand where the economy was heading and for how long this crisis would last.

The first sign that started to worry Henry was a noticeable drop in customers at the garage. People couldn't afford to drive their cars as much and couldn't afford to repair them. It wasn't long till the mechanics at the garage had nothing to do. Henry could see the handwriting on the wall, but he elected not to share his fears with Ella. Less than a week later Dave called Henry into his office. Dave was obviously distraught as he informed Henry he had to lay him off work. Dave was keeping Andrew on for the few customers they had left but everyone else, he had to let go.

That night after supper Henry told Ella what was happening. He told her first thing the next morning he would go looking for another job. Henry still didn't grasp the magnitude of the depression's effect. There were no jobs. Day after day Henry walked the streets just like thousands of others in search of work that just wasn't there. What little savings they had started to dwindle. The church helped its parishioners out from time to time with a few food items, but the help was short-lived. Henry was growing desperate. One day while walking the streets he picked up a magazine lying on the sidewalk. When he got back to his house, he flipped through the pages. On the second to last page was a small ad that read: "Pilots and airplane mechanics needed for a crop dusting business in the plains of Kansas." There was no phone number with the ad, just the name of the town, Anomie, Kansas. Henry knew the ad might be a hoax. Even if it wasn't, the job would probably be filled before they could get there. In his mind, he weighed those thoughts against the job availability in New York. This town that he had grown to love just didn't have anything to offer him at this time. Could it be any worse there than it currently was here? That night after Brooks went to sleep, Henry asked Ella her thoughts about possibly leaving New York.

Ella pondered it for a few moments then said, "The idea of leaving this place really scares me. We've gotten to know so many people around here, I wish we didn't have to start over. But Henry, I know you are a man that has to work, and there's no work here. Once before we made a decision to move and the good Lord took care of us. If we move again, you know He'll be with us." They hugged. They talked about the things they had to do before leaving and all the people they needed to contact. The next morning Henry told Andrew and Dave they were moving.

Dave said, "I'm so sorry Henry. If there was any-thing, I could do." Andrew took it the hardest. Henry was like a brother to him. The thought of not getting to watch Brooks grow up was really going to eat Andrew up. Andrew told Henry if he found work in the Midwest that he should write to him. He might move to. Sunday morning the Borgmans told the minister who announced it to the congregation. After church, everyone expressed how sad they were at seeing them leave, but they all wished them the best of luck. All over America, this same scene was being played out again and again. City people heading for the country hoping to find a life of sustenance at the very least. While country folks packed their bags and went to the cities believing that there had to be work amongst all those buildings. The government did the best they could to create projects and jobs to help some people, but in reality, help was just going to take some time. As for Henry and Ella, their time to try something new was now.

Chapter 4
SOME NICE STRANGERS

Henry and Ella packed up some food items for the trip along with their clothes, pictures and mementos. They were able to sell a few small things to raise some extra cash to use as gas money. The one item left was the homemade baby cradle that the church had given them. Even though they could've gotten some money for it, they decided to give it back to the church in the hopes they would find someone else who could use it. Wednesday morning the Borgman's old sedan left the buildings of New York and headed for the plains of Kansas. Henry and Ella had discussed the fact that the job in Kansas was likely no longer there. So they made it a point that every town they drove through they would look for help wanted ads. Every time they stopped for gas they asked about the availability of jobs in that area. The answers were always the same. They would pull off the road occasionally and eat some meals from the food they had brought along. Ella took turns driving, but sometimes they just had to park the car and sleep. Brooks was antsy, as any four-year-old would be, but Ella did the best she could to keep him entertained with road games and coloring books. They blew out their second tire of the trip just west of St. Louis. Having already used the spare Henry wasn't sure if they had enough money to buy another tire. Once again, fate smiled on the Borgmans. A kindly old farmer stopped by and asked if he could help. Henry explained his predicament and told the farmer he was about out of money. The old farmer said, "You know the good book says to do unto others, as you would have them do unto you. I reckon if I had a flat tire, I would hope somebody would help me. I think the spare on my pickup will fit your car. You give me one of your blown-out tires and rims, and I'll put another tire on it when I get home."

Henry changed the tire, and both he and Ella thanked the man for his kindness, then they were on their way again. Another day and they were rolling into the quaint little town of Anomie, Kansas. Henry and Ella guessed the picturesque community held two or three hundred residents. Most of the streets were lined with large shade trees which was a stark contrast to the open prairies they had driven through the last 50 miles or so. The gas tank on Henry's car was almost empty. As was his wallet. And he hoped that the crop dusting business was close by and that they were still looking for help. Henry parked on the street next to the service station and went to ask some folks where the business might be. As you might expect, when a stranger driving a car with a New York license plate pulls into town, he's met with a good deal of suspicion. Henry explained that he had seen an ad looking for a mechanic. He was hoping a job might still be available. George was the man's name who ran the service station, and he told Henry he didn't think the crop dusting service needed any more help. "But if you want to talk to Tom, you'll find him right on the west edge of town." Henry thanked George and returned to his car. The Borgmans rolled up to the airfield and parked outside the hangar by a door with a sign over it that read "Office."

Henry nervously looked at Ella who was cradling the sleeping Brooks and said, "Wish me luck."

Henry went in through the already open door and met a tall, distinguished looking gentleman who was wiping his hands on a shop towel. He asked, "Can I help you?"

Henry replied, "A while back I saw an ad that you might be looking for a mechanic. I was wondering if that position was still available."

"Are you an inspector or a government man of some kind?"

"No sir. I'm just an out of work mechanic looking for a job."

Brooks had woken up, so he and Ella stepped out of the car to stretch their legs. Tom, who was looking Henry up and down, saw the mom and her son emerge from the car and his fears of Henry being some kind of inspector ebbed somewhat. He continued, "So you say you're an airplane mechanic?"

"Well, I am a pretty good mechanic, but I've never actually worked on planes before."

Tom shook his head, "I'm sorry. I might be able to use somebody, but I really need someone with airplane engine experience. I hope you understand."

Henry jumped in, "I'm a fast learner. I know I could catch on quickly."

Tom shook his head again, "I'm sorry. I just can't be paying someone and teaching them at the same time. You'll have to excuse me." Tom went back into the main part of the hangar.

Henry's mind was numb. He had placed all his remaining hopes on getting this job. He shuffled back to the car. He didn't have to say anything, Ella could already tell. Henry picked up Brooks and held him tightly.

Ella placed her hand on her husband's arm and said, "It'll be all right. Something good is bound to happen soon. Maybe I can find some kind of work."

Henry continued to silently stare at the horizon. Even though Tom had walked into the main part of the hangar, he continued to keep an eye on the Borgmans as they huddled near their car. Tom wished he could help but times were tough here too. Tom watched as Henry placed Brooks back on the ground, then turned and headed back for Tom's office. Tom met him there. His voice was cracking as Henry told Tom, "I'll work for free."

Tom was a little taken back, "What?"

Henry repeated, "I'll work for free until you deem that I'm worthy of a salary."

"But don't you need money now?"

"I'll sell the car for what I can get. Maybe I can make that last until I get a paycheck."

Tom had his business side, but he was also a compassionate man. He thought for a moment then took a deep breath, "All right. You can work here for no pay till I determine what kind of mechanic you are."

A bit of a smile broke out on Henry's lips as he stuck out his hand, "Thank you."

Tom returned the handshake and asked, "You're thanking me for not paying you?"

"No," Henry replied. "I'm thanking you for giving me a chance."

Henry returned to the car to tell Ella. His mind was whirling about what they would do when he sold the car. Henry informed Ella that Tom was going to give him a chance. Before he could tell Ella any more, Tom walked up beside them.

"When's the last time you and your family had something to eat?"

Before Henry or Ella could answer, Brooks broke in, "We had some crackers this morning. But I'm kind of hungry again."

Tom laughed. He bent over placing his hands on his knees so he could look Brooks in the face, "Well you see that little diner over there? They've got some of the best food around. And you really have to try their cherry pie."

Brooks's eyes lit up at the thought of a full meal.

Henry and Ella didn't know how to tell Tom they didn't have any money. Tom straightened back up and spoke before Henry and Ella could. "My sister owns that place. You folks go get something to eat, and I'll call and tell her to put it on my tab. Oh, and also there's a little two-room apartment behind the diner.... You can stay there till you find something better."

Ella placed her hands over her face in a burst of emotion. Henry momentarily bowed his head then looked back up and stuck out his hand, "Thank you! I'll pay you back."

Tom laughed as he replied, "You dang right you will! I'm going to make you an airplane mechanic."

Henry was wearing his biggest smile in weeks, "Oh I almost forgot. My name's Henry. Henry Borgman. This is my wife Ella and our son Brooks."

Tom shook Brooks his hand, "Brooks, I'm glad to meet you. My name is Tom Shaw."

Ella took her hands off her face and startled Tom when she gave him a big hug. "Thank you. Thank you so much. Last night I prayed that the good Lord with send someone to help us. It's you. I think he sent you."

Tom, somewhat embarrassed, held up his hands, "Whoa! I'm sure the good Lord has better people that he can send than me. But I do consider myself a pretty good judge of character and I kind of think you folks might be a good fit for our little town. Now go get something to eat. That cherry pie might be getting cold."

Tom may have very well been sent by the good Lord. Who knows? But the fact that the Borgmans made another major change in their lives and landed back on their feet was for real. At this time they couldn't possibly know how important Anomie, Kansas and its residents would become to them. Nor could they know the vital part that would be written in the history books because of them living here. Right now the cherry pie was delicious.... The à la mode was on the house.

Chapter 5
A Real Job

Tom's sister's name was Alice. She almost immediately became close friends with the Borgmans. Over the years she and Ella would become like sisters. After just a few weeks, Alice asked Brooks to call her aunt Alice. Alice, who was a few years older than Ella, never married. She always told Ella she didn't have time to care for a man at her house because she was too busy taking care of half the men in town when they were at the diner. Ella would be quick to tell anyone that Alice was one of the nicest and friendliest people you could ever meet.

The very next morning after arriving in Anomie, Henry was waiting at the hangar door when Tom showed up for work. "Man. It looks like you're ready to go," said Tom.

Henry, pointed to one of the planes and replied,

"I'm just anxious to find out what keeps these things in the air."

"Well Henry, in not too long, hopefully, you'll be the reason these things stay in the air."

The two men laughed as Tom opened the unlocked office door. Henry was a little surprised that the door was unlocked and asked Tom, "Aren't you afraid someone might break in here?"

"Ah, Henry. To tell you the truth if I ran a car dealership, I might lock the doors cause anybody in town could drive a car away. But there's only two guys here that can fly a plane, and I'm one of them, so if a plane goes missing, I've got a pretty good suspect in mind." Henry laughed as he followed Tom into the hangar.

"Tom. I do want to get started learning airplane engines. But could I ask you a little bit about your business?"

"Sure," said Tom.

"Well, it's just that driving into town I noticed most of the land was prairie. A lot of pasture and a few wheat fields. What exactly do you spray around here?"

"Good question Henry. Coming into town the way you did, it is mostly prairie. But the town is kinda located on the start of a river basin that runs to the north. The dirt's a lot better that way, and there are a lot of vegetables grown there, as well as a couple of really big orchards. A couple of miles outside of town, there is a pretty big canning plant. A lot of the folks from town work there. We stay pretty busy here trying to keep the bugs from eatin' up all the profits."

Henry nodded, "That sounds really interesting.

Hopefully one of these days I can take Ella and Brooks on a drive out that way."

"Shoot," said Tom. "We'll just take a drive out there this evening after work. But for right now, it's time for you to go to school."

Henry smiled, "I'm ready to start learnin'."

Tom was the sole owner of Shaw's Dusters. His business provided a vital service to the fruit and vegetable industry in the area. He also sprayed fields for the local farmers as the need arose. Obviously, his business here in Kansas was seasonal, so on occasion, he would fly his planes as far south as Mexico to help with spraying down there during the Kansas winters. Tom owned two Stearman bi-winged planes fitted with Pratt and Whitney Wasp Junior engines. The nine-cylinder radial engines produced around three hundred horsepower. These two planes were Tom's pride and joy, and he didn't trust just anybody working on them. Henry was quick to see how meticulous Tom was in the service and maintenance of his planes. As Tom began Henry's instruction on how these engines worked. Henry began to fear that maybe he was overmatched by these mechanical marvels.

Along about midmorning, a little older gentleman strolled into the hangar. Tom introduced Henry to Gene Telford, Tom's other pilot. The three men chatted for a bit, then Tom told Gene to take the one plane and head for Hackman's orchard. Gene gave Tom a little salute and said, "You got it, Boss." Tom and Henry watched from the hangar door as Gene fired up his plane and headed north. Tom told Henry that

Gene had been a fighter pilot during world war one. He had shot down a couple of German planes during the war, and one time he saw the German ace, the Red Baron, in the air. On that occasion, both Gene and the Red Baron were out of ammunition, and they simply waved to each other as they headed back to their respective lines. Henry was impressed with this bit of knowledge and hope someday he could sit and talk to Gene a while.

By five o'clock that first afternoon, Henry's head was swimming with new information about airplane engines. Tom assured him that he would catch on and Henry hoped that Tom's faith in him was justified. Tom told Henry, "That's enough for one day. Why don't you go get Ella and Brooks and meet me back here in about a half hour? I'll go get my wife and will take a little drive through the valley." Tom and his wife Debbie were waiting for the Borgmans when they got back to the hangar. Debbie was just as nice and friendly as everyone else the Borgmans had met in this town. Turns out Debbie taught the first four grades at the local grade school. In a year, Brooks would be in her classroom. The two couples and Brooks had a very pleasant ride that evening as the Borgmans tried to take in all the wonderful views in this wide open country. A mile or two after driving out of Anomie, the orchards came into view.

Henry gave out a little whistle, then said to Brooks, "Brooks, look at all those fruit trees." Then turning to Tom, he asked, "What kind of fruit is grown here?"

Tom replied, "Well Henry, there's a lot of apple

trees, but there are also pears, plums, and cherries."

Brooks piped up, "You mean like for cherry pie?"

Everyone laughed as Tom answered, "Yup Brooks. Especially for cherry pie." A little further on they saw the vegetable fields. This drive in the country was wonderful. Only a couple of days living in Kansas and Henry and Ella confided in the Shaw's that they felt they were going to like this even better than New York. Henry and Ella learned that Tom and Debbie had two daughters, eighteen and twenty years old. Both girls had already headed to college for the upcoming year. The Shaws dropped the Borgmans off at their little apartment, and Henry and Ella repeatedly thanked the Shaw's for the tour and the pleasant evening.

Henry told Tom, "I'll see you in the morning and tomorrow I won't wait for you to unlock the door."

Both men laughed as Henry closed the back door on Tom's car. Brooks piped up, "Can we have some more cherry pie?" Henry and Ella laughed as they headed for the diner's front door.

Henry told Ella, "I'd better get this job if I'm going to have any chance of paying off Brooks's diner tab." They followed Brooks through the door. "Hey Alice. Any cherry pie left?"

The next couple days Henry continued to learn about airplanes and their engines. By Thursday afternoon a few things were starting to click in Henry's mind. A little after five, Brooks walked into the hangar where Henry and Tom were talking. Tom was taking a real liking to Brooks, and he didn't mind the boy being around the hangar, as long as he didn't touch too much stuff. Just after Brooks arrived at the hangar, Gene landed his plane after another day of dusting. When Gene walked into the hangar and joined the other three, he reached down and gave Brooks a pinch on the ribs. "How you doin' there squirt?" was Gene's question.

In mid-laugh Brooks answered, "Fine."

Tom inquired of Gene, "How did it go today?"

"Oh, it was fine," came the reply. "But the thing is still a little doggie when you're loaded and trying to pull up on that sharp rise on the east end."

"Yah," said Tom. "I'm not quite sure how to give the engine a little boost without floodin' it out."

Gene jokingly said as he pointed towards Henry, "Just tell the new guy to have that problem fixed by morning."

Everybody laughed as Gene said he was calling it a day and he headed for his car.

Henry told Tom, "I didn't think these engines would ever run short of power."

"Well," replied Tom. "It's not that bad. But I just wish we could get a little more umph when we're coming up out of a pass. I could give it a little more fuel, but I'm afraid of flooding it out. We can live with it."

"You might as well head out Henry," Tom said he was heading home also.

"If it's okay with you," asked Henry, "I might hang around and read up in a few more of these service manuals?"

"Suit yourself," said Tom. "But when you leave just remember to lock up just the way I would." They laughed, and Tom strolled on out to his car.

Henry told Brooks he should probably go back to the apartment. "Your mom will be looking for you."

Brooks replied, "No she won't. She sent me over here because one of Alice's waitresses got sick, so mom is helping Alice."

"Well okay. But I've got some reading I want to do so I need you to keep pretty quiet. Okay?"

"Okay," was Brooks's answer.

And Brooks was pretty quiet for an hour or so as Henry studied the service guides reading about the fuel supply and how it was delivered to the wasp engine. Finally, Brooks's quiet button was worn out, and he began to ask questions of his dad.

"Why are you readin' that book dad?"

"I'm trying to learn more about these airplane engines."

"What's a matter with them?"

"Well, there's nothing really a matter with them. It's just that sometimes they could run better if they had a little more gas."

"Why don't you just run another gas hose to the motor?"

As Henry was preparing to deflect Brooks's inquiry, the simplicity of Brooks's question made Henry asked himself, "Yeah, why couldn't we run another gas line to the motor?"

Henry laid down the service manual, picked up a flashlight and walked over to the one plane that was in the hanger. He studied long and hard on the idea of another supply line. After a while, he went back to the office to read some more. Brooks had lain down on the couch and was now fast asleep. Henry sat down in the one recliner in the office and began to read.

After Ella got done helping Alice cleanup at the diner, she prepared to go to the apartment. Then she noticed the office lights still on at the hangar. She walked across the parking lot and through the open office door. She found Brooks sleeping on the couch and Henry sleeping in the recliner with the service manual resting on his chest. She didn't know whether to wake them or let them sleep. She decided to let them sleep where they were, and she went back to the apartment by herself.

When Tom came into the office the next morning, he found Henry and Brooks right were Ella had left them. Henry woke up when he smelled the pot of coffee that Tom had put on.

"Oh man. I'm sorry," said Henry. "I didn't mean to sleep in your office."

"Hey. That's no problem," answered Tom. I just thought maybe Ella threw both of you men out."

Henry laughed as he looked over at Brooks who was trying to rub the sleep out of his eyes as well.

Tom continued as he pointed to the service manual Henry was holding. "You must have found something pretty interesting in there to keep you here all night."

"Well," said Henry. "Something Brooks said last night got me thinking. He said why don't you just run another gas line to the motor."

"Gas hose," corrected Brooks.

"Okay. Gas hose. Don't get me wrong Tom. I know

it's not that simple, but I was trying to figure out if there could be a little auxiliary fuel supply that would be available to the engine and regulated by a governor or something."

Tom thought for a second and said, "You know Henry, that makes a lot of sense, but I'm afraid that's more than me, or you can answer. I think it's time to call the big boys over in Wichita. That's where those engines are made. Why don't you go check on your wife and get this junior mechanic some breakfast. Maybe when you come back, they will have given me an idea we can try."

As Henry and Brooks headed across the parking lot, they saw Ella coming their way. She was just going to check on them. The three enjoyed eating their breakfast together, then Ella and Brooks returned to the apartment and Henry went back to Tom's office. Tom had a big smile on his face as he was just hanging up the phone.

"Henry. Your idea is pretty much right on the money. Pratt and Whitney makes a kit we can add on that pretty much does just what you said. They said other customers have had the same problem and this kit should clear it right up. Good thinking Henry."

"I guess you have to thank Brooks."

"I kinda think Brooks has some natural instincts from a father who's a pretty good mechanic."

"I hope you're right."

"Before you leave today, make sure you fill out one of these employment pages. I need to have that before I can write you a paycheck."

Henry swallowed hard to keep the lump in his throat from rising too high. He asked, "You mean like, whenever I get good enough to deserve a paycheck?"

"No. I mean like right now. If you promise me that you won't quit learnin', then I promise you that you'll always have a job. Agreed?"

Henry was in heaven! He had a paying job.

Chapter 6
A NEW HOMETOWN

Henry wanted to run right over to Ella and tell her the news, but he stayed at work and helped Tom with whatever he could. When 5 o'clock rolled around, Henry thanked Tom for probably the tenth time that day, then headed back to the apartment to share his good news with Ella and Brooks. He told Ella that he was so incredibly happy to have a job, but at the same time, he was a little scared. Tom was being so nice to him, hiring him and all, that he didn't want to let Tom down.

Ella said, "Don't worry honey. Tom knows that you're not an airplane mechanic yet. But in the few days you guys have been together, Tom sees in you the qualities of a good worker and a good friend. He's not going to give up on you so don't you go giving up on yourself."

Henry smiled and gave Ella a kiss on the cheek. "I won't. Thanks."

The next day was Saturday and Tom's business didn't work on Saturdays or Sundays except in emergencies. Tom had actually given Henry a little check for some spending money, so Henry, Ella, and Brooks decided to go cash the check and do a walking tour of their new town. Word of mouth travels fast in these communities and most people they met on the street already knew the Henry was working for Tom Shaw. Anomie, Kansas was pretty much an exact opposite of New York City. Anomie had one gas station, one bank, one grocery store, two hardware stores, a feed store, a newspaper, a barbershop/beauty salon and one church. As Henry, Ella, and Brooks stopped in front of the church, they read the name on the sign. Trinity Lutheran Church. Ella clutched Henry's arm, "Henry! It's the same as in New York! I really do believe we were meant to be here."

The next morning the Borgmans went to church. They introduced themselves to the minister, Reverend Jedediah Foster, who graciously welcomed them to the church and to the community. They sat down in an empty pew but momentarily were joined by Tom and Debbie Shaw on one side and Alice Shaw on the other side. Alice slid in next to Ella and gave her a little hug. She whispered, "I'm so glad you guys are here."

Henry gave a little wave to Gene Telford as he went down the aisle as well as George from the gas station.

When the service started one of the first things Reverend Foster did was to introduce the Borgmans to the whole congregation. The Borgmans stood up, and kind of bowed but they were also a little embarrassed. When church ended, it seemed like every single one of the hundred and fifty or so members shook the Borgman's hands and welcome them to Anomie. When the crowd finally dispersed, and the folks headed for home, Henry, Ella and Brooks headed back to their apartment as well. They walked along in silence first as the family was taking in the true splendor of this little town. Henry broke the silence, "The Lord sure works in mysterious ways. Doesn't he?" Ella didn't say anything. She just smiled and rested her head against Henry's arm. The Borgmans stopped at the grocery which was open till noon and picked up a few things so they wouldn't keep running up a tab at Alice's diner.

When they were back in New York, it seemed that fate was trying to crush the Borgman's American dream, but somehow they slipped through the fingers of the Great Depression and found a beautiful place to live and watch their son grow up. At this point in history, the Borgman's future looked much brighter than for most Americans. For Henry and Ella, Anomie was their slice of cherry pie.... Brooks was the à la mode.

Chapter 7
Buying The Farm

Life for the Borgman family had settled into a nice routine. Henry worked for Tom and continued to get more and more comfortable with the work he did on the planes. Ella worked for Alice in the diner five days a week in the evenings. It was only a matter of weeks before Tom told Henry his tab at the diner and apartment was paid in full. Since Alice actually owned the apartment, she took her rent money out of Ella's paycheck. Ella always told Alice she wasn't charging them enough, but Alice insisted she was getting all the rent she wanted. Time kind of flew by, and it wasn't long until the Borgmans had lived in Anomie for a year. Henry had caught on fairly quickly to the service requirements of the airplanes. Tom still called the shots on anything major, but he was trusting Henry's judgment more and more. With Henry handling most things in the shop, Tom had more time to fly and to keep up with the books. The business was running smoothly. The little apartment was nice, and it was handy for Henry and Ella's jobs. But with Brooks growing bigger and now that they had a few dollars saved up Henry and Ella agreed that it was time to look for a little larger place to live. Since coming to America, all the Borgmans had done was rent their homes. They assumed that they could find a bigger house to rent somewhere in town. But when they started looking, they found out the only couple of houses for rent were in really bad shape. One Saturday morning when Henry took his paycheck into the bank, the bank's vice president, Harold Jones, asked Henry to come into his office. Henry had met Mr. Jones at church, and he seemed like a very nice man, but Henry was a little nervous about being asked into his office. Harold closed the door and told Henry to have a seat.

Harold started, "Well Henry, your family has lived here for more than a year now. How do you like our little town?"

Henry replied, "Oh, it's wonderful. I never knew that a whole town could be so nice. We really love it here."

"That's good. Good. Well, the reason I asked you in here, I heard you were looking for a house to rent."

"Yeah, that's right."

"I may have something better for you. That little farm place on the north side of town belonged to widow Martin who passed away last month. The bank had a lien on that place and well, long story short, the bank ended up with the property. There's about ten acres of ground that goes with that house and barn, and I know it needs a little bit of work, but the banks not asking that much for the place and I think you and your family would be a perfect fit for that little farm."

This idea caught Henry by surprise. "Well Mr. Jones, we don't have much money saved up yet. I don't think that there's any way we can buy a place right now."

"Please Henry. Just call me Harold. If you just put a few hundred dollars down on the place, the bank will hold the rest on a mortgage. I think that would be a great place to raise that boy of yours."

Henry's head was swimming. He and Ella had never owned anything their whole married life except the car. He thought for a moment then replied, "I have to tell you. The idea of owning my own home is kind of exciting. But I have to talk this over with Ella. Can we maybe go see the place sometime?"

"I'll tell you what Henry. The bank closes at noon. I'll run home and grab a bite of lunch and why don't you and Ella and Brooks meet me there about one o'clock?"

"Wow," said Henry. "This is all kind of sudden, but I guess it won't hurt to look. Okay, we'll meet you there."

"Great. See you at one."

When Henry got back to the apartment and told Ella, her first reaction was there was no way they could afford to buy a home. Then she said, "I'm sure we can't do that right now. But Henry, whenever we went past that place, it reminded me of my parents' little farm back in Germany. You don't suppose that we could do this? Do you?"

"I don't know Ella. I suppose we'll just go look at the place and see what kind of numbers Harold throws at us."

When they arrived at one, Harold was there waiting.

"Hey, Henry and Ella. How are you doing young man?" Harold asked as he shook Brooks's hand. "Ella, I was telling Henry we think you guys would be the perfect fit for this property. The house is good and solid. It just needs a little paint and some love. The barn would shape right up with a new coat of paint, and there's that little pasture that would be perfect for a couple of cows or something. I'm told that the pond has a lot of fish in it and come fall, those oak trees in the backyard are said to be loaded with squirrels. Not a bad place for a young boy to grow up in. Is it?"

"Oh please," answered Henry. "You don't have to sell us on the aesthetics of the place. We already love all of that. It comes down to what's inside the house and how much is this going to cost us."

Harold opened the door to the house and let the Borgmans inside. What they saw inside took their breath away. Though the house was dusty and musty from sitting idle, it was instantly evident to the Borgmans this was a special home. The house was twice as big as the home they rented in New York. There was handcrafted woodwork above all the doors and the mantle and the open staircase to the second floor was fantastic.

Even though Ella fell instantly in love with the home, she kept her thoughts to herself for fear of getting her hopes up too high before they heard the price. Henry was equally enamored with the place and felt they better leave now before he grew so attached that he wouldn't be able to say no when they heard the cost. The group went back outside into the front porch. Harold told Henry and Ella to try out the swing that hung there. They both knew they shouldn't. Their love for the place was already going to cloud their judgment. They sat down. Without saying anything to one another, they both knew that this could be a place they could love for the rest of their lives. Harold and Brooks sat down on the porch floor.

Harold spoke. "Well. Do you like the place?" Henry and Ella looked at each other then back at Harold and nodded yes.

"Henry, since you and your family arrived here, I haven't talked to a single person that doesn't like you folks. Tom Shaw's the guy who told me you were looking for a house. Me and the rest of the bank board think it's important for our town to keep young families like yourselves living here for a long time. When the bank received this property, Mrs. Martin owed about twenty thousand dollars on the place. The bank figured if we cleaned it up and advertised a little, we might get thirty or forty thousand for it. But money can't buy folks like yourselves. So if you want this place you can have it for the twenty thousand that Mrs. Martin still owed."

Henry's mind was whirling. He had no idea how he could afford that much debt, but he was fully expecting the bank to ask twice that much. Ella's eyes grew large as she looked first at Harold then back at Henry. "Is there any way we can do that?"

Harold interrupted, "Before you answer Henry, I need to tell you more. Ordinarily, the bank would want ten or twenty percent of the money in advance. But like I said we want you guys to have this house. The bank will make you a loan for 20 years. In lieu of the down payment, Tom Shaw told us he would cosign the bank loan for you. You guys give us your signatures, we'll give you the house."

Ella had tears, and Henry was choked up. "I...I can't ask Tom to do that."

"Henry. Tom is one of our best bank customers. He wouldn't have offered his signature unless he really thought a lot of your family. Tom told me he wasn't one bit worried that you folks would pay back every last penny on the loan. Do me, the bank, Tom, this town and yourselves a favor. Take the house."

Henry inhaled a long deep breath as he looked into Ella's eyes. "Well, honey. I guess we're going to be homeowners."

Ella threw her arms around Henry and kissed him. Then she rose from the swing and hugged Harold. She wiped the moisture from her eyes and told Harold, "When I see Tom, first I'm going to tell him that he's too nice for his own good. Then I'm going to hug him to pieces."

Everyone laughed, even as the Borgmans were reeling in their minds over what just happened.

Harold told them to come to the bank the following Saturday, and he would have all the papers ready to sign. Harold got in his car and left. The Borgmans were still stunned, and they weren't sure whether to stay there or go back to the apartment. Finally, they left. They had a lot to think about this next week. Praise the Lord!

When they got back to their little apartment, Ella hurried into the diner to tell Alice. When Ella came through the door, Alice looked up and started grinning from ear to ear. "So," she began, "did you like the house?"

Ella put her hands on her hips, "You knew about this too?"

"Heck Ella, in this little town people know pretty much everything about everybody. Tom told me you guys were going to look at it. He said he was going to try and help along your decision."

"Well, he certainly did that. All of you people are just too nice. I don't know how we can ever repay you."

"Ella, Tom really does like your family, but he's co-signed loans for other people as well. Financially he's doing fine and feels like he's been really blessed. He just wants to share some of those blessings with other folks. If he thought you were going to skip out on him, he wouldn't have done it."

"Well," replied Ella, "I'm going to miss walking twenty steps to go to work, but I can't wait to get in that house."

Ella gave Alice a hug and headed to the apartment.

Chapter 8
A Straight Shooter

The Borgmans arrived at church a little early the next morning. They wanted to thank Tom once again for his kindness. When the worship service was underway, Reverend Foster asked the congregation if there were any prayer wishes. Henry stood up.

Reverend Foster smiled, "Yes Henry."

Henry was kind of emotional as he spoke, "Well Reverend, I just wanted to say, Ella, Brooks and I have lived here for a little over a year now. Quite possibly it's been the best year of my life. I never knew that a whole community could be so friendly and kind. And, well, we just wanted to tell everyone thanks and if there is ever anything that we can do for you, well, just ask. Thank you."

Reverend Foster was smiling even more when he replied. "You know Henry, the Bible tells us to treat others the way that we would like to be treated. My experience tells me that you and your family are wonderful people. I think the folks here are just returning the kindness you have shown them. However," the reverends grin turned into a sly look, "if you meant what you said about offering to help…the church council will be looking for a new trustee this year."

The congregation broke out in laughter. Henry and Ella were laughing right with them. Henry stood back up. "Well, I can't think of anyone who owes the Lord more than I do. If the church wants me, I'll be happy to do it." Some of the congregation applauded.

Tom Shaw shouted out, "I move the nominations be closed." More laughter followed.

Reverend Foster said, "Wonderful! Just wonderful. But we better get moving along with our service. If I don't start my sermon pretty soon, you folks won't get home in time for dinner."

Year number two in the town of Anomie was off to a fast start for the Borgmans. They signed the papers at the bank and all their spare time for the next month or so was spent getting their new home ready. The house looked fantastic with its new coat of paint and Ella had the inside spick and span. There were a few old pieces of furniture that went with the house and some of the townsfolk offered other pieces that the Borgmans could have. Since they didn't own anything while living in the apartment, the actual move only involved their clothes and a few personal items. Less than two months after closing on it, the Borgmans spent their first night in their new home. Even though this home was so important to Henry and Ella, the person that got the most benefit out of it was Brooks. Living on the edge of town with all the fishing, hunting and hiking you could want was a dream come true for a growing boy.

When Brooks wasn't in school, he was usually in the woods. Sometimes with some of his friends. Henry had never been much of a hunter, but he always loved to fish. As Brooks continued to grow, he and his father fished not only their little pond but most all the creeks and rivers in the area. Bass, catfish, bluegill. They were all fair game, and the father-son duo provided a lot of delicious meals over the years.

Since Henry now drove his car to work most days, Brooks would often walk to the hanger after school to catch a ride home with his dad. He didn't come out and say it, but Brooks really enjoyed hearing the stories the men had to tell when quitting time was drawing near. Brooks had tagged along behind Gene a few times squirrel hunting, but he was really wishing that someday he would have his own rifle to hunt with. One day at the hanger as Brooks stood between Tom and Henry, Gene asked him, "How old are you now Brooks?"

"I'm ten, goin' on eleven."

"Man, you kids really do grow up fast. Henry, when are you going to buy this boy a 22 rifle?"

Henry was kind of taken back by the question. "Well, I guess I never thought too much about it. I never hunted much myself. What do you think? Is Brooks ready for a gun?"

"Heck yes," came Gene's reply. "There's kids his age around town that been shootin' 22's for a couple of years already. Tomorrow's Saturday. I'll bring a rifle to your place tomorrow afternoon, and me and you and Brooks can shoot up some tin cans in that pasture of yours. Okay?"

"Yah, sure, that's fine with me. As long as Brooks wants to." Brooks didn't have to reply, his expression said it all.

"Good, I'll see ya tomorrow."

Tom joined in. "Well I'm coming by to watch, and I'll bet you two a dollar that Brooks out shoots both of you."

Henry and Brooks laughed as Gene told Tom, "You're on."

It would be hard for Brooks to get to sleep that night. When Henry and Brooks stopped the car in front of the house, Brooks rushed in to tell his mom. "Guess what? Gene's coming over tomorrow to help teach me how to shoot a 22 rifle."

By the time Brooks told his mother this, Henry had arrived in the kitchen, fully expecting to hear Ella oppose this idea. But to his surprise, Ella was all for it. "Oh, I think that's wonderful. Gene is so nice. I know your father never did much hunting but back in Germany, my father and brothers hunted all the time. I think it's an important thing for you to know."

With his mother's approval, Brooks was on cloud nine.

Next afternoon, Gene and Tom rolled up to the Borgman's house in Gene's old clunker of a car. Brooks flew out to the car to meet them. "You ready to plunk a few cans?" Gene asked.

"You bet," came Brooks says reply. "I already set up a bunch of cans on that old board fence behind the barn."

"Perfect," said Gene.

Tom jumped in, "Remember Brooks, I'm counting on you to help me get that dollar from Gene."

"Well, I'll do my best," said Brooks.

As Brooks, Gene and Tom started to head to the barn, they were joined by Henry and Ella.

Ella put her hand on Gene's shoulder, "Oh Gene. This is so nice of you to help teach Brooks how to shoot."

"Think nothin' of it," was his reply. "It's time that boy helped me put it dent in the squirrel population around here."

When the five of them rounded the corner of the barn, they saw about one hundred cans sitting atop the old fence.

"Holy cats Brooks! Where did you find all them cans?"

"There was a couple of big bags of empty cans in the barn. I guess that older lady must have been saving them for something."

Gene laughed. "You might have more cans than I have bullets. But we should have some fun."

Gene then got more serious as he started instructing Brooks about how a gun works and the precautions you take handling a weapon. Ella was glad Gene was taking the time to show Brooks so much about the rifle. When she looked at Henry, she realized Henry was taking in as much as Brooks was. When Gene felt Brooks was ready, he handed him the empty gun. He showed him how to hold the gun and aim. Brooks was patient because he knew how important all this information was. But his heart jumped a little bit when Gene announced, "I think you're ready to give it a try."

Gene gave Brooks one bullet and watched as Brooks loaded the gun the way he had shown him. He took careful aim and fired. Miss. As was the second shot. And the third. Gene smiled and reassured Brooks, "You're doin' fine. You're shooting right over the tops of those cans. You need to get your cheek down on the stock a little more. Put that bead right down in the bottom of that vee and squeeze the trigger. Don't jerk it."

Shot number four brought the ringing sound of metal as a soup can disappeared from the fence.

A shout of approval went up from the four spectators as Brooks grinned from ear to ear. From that point on the hit's got more regular and the misses got farther and farther apart. For the rest of the afternoon, the group took turns, even Ella, at plunking the cans off of the fence.

By the end of the day, Brooks was showing the makings of being a pretty good shot. The group went back to Gene's car, and Brooks thanked Gene for like the tenth time. "Maybe when the next squirrel season rolls around, I'll have a gun of my own, and me and you can hunt together," he told Gene.

Gene was quiet for a few seconds, then spoke. "You

already have a gun. I want you to have this one. If it's okay with your mom and dad?"

Brooks whirled around staring wide-eyed at his parents.

Henry said, "Oh Gene. We can't ask you to do that."

"Please Henry. I want to. My wife's been gone almost ten years now. My daughter lives in St. Louis. Spending time with Brooks means a lot to me. I've got more guns at the house and well...seein' the boy get all excited about it kinda reminds me of when I was his age. Besides, I need a huntin' partner and Tom here just makes too much noise walking through the woods."

Everyone laughed as Tom gave Gene a friendly shove.

Henry and Ella looked at each other then Henry turned back to Brooks. "Well, Brooks. I guess it's okay with your mom and I, but you really owe Mr. Telford. Any time he's got any chores to do I want you to go help him. Understood?"

"Yes sir! Thanks, Mom, thanks Dad, and especially thanks to you Gene. I'll take good care of your gun."

"Your gun."

"Okay.... My gun."

The arrival of that little rifle in Brooks's life would actually start a chain of events and ultimately would help write a chapter in American history. Every fall and winter, Brooks, Gene and Henry, who also fell in love with hunting, would hunt squirrels and rabbits while providing themselves with fun and memories as well as adding a lot of meat to the dinner table. A couple of years after giving Brooks the rifle, Gene also gave him a pump-action shotgun. Now the little hunting group added quail, doves, ducks and geese to the table fare. The shotgun was especially important in Brooks's life because Gene taught him the art of leading a moving target. Gene always told him, "Don't shoot where he is, shoot where he's gonna be when your bullet arrives." Brooks showed a natural ability to figure this out, and in no time he was outshooting Gene in bird hunting.

Even though Henry was and always would be the most important man in his life, Brooks was blessed by having men around him who loved to share their time and knowledge with him.

Chapter 9
LEARNING TO FLY

When Brooks was 13, Tom asked Henry if he could take Brooks on an airplane ride with him. Even though Henry worked on the planes, he himself wasn't all that anxious to ride in one. But Henry said if Brooks wants to go, that is fine with him. Brooks about jumped out of his shoes at the opportunity to go. When Tom and Brooks landed after that first flight, Henry could see that same look in his son's eyes that he saw in the eyes of Tom and Gene. Brooks was hooked on flying. From that moment on, Brooks took every opportunity that came along to ride with Tom and also with Gene. One day Tom had to fly to the city to pick up a part for the canning factory. He asked Brooks if he wanted to go along. Brooks immediately answered yes then looked at Henry. "If it's okay with dad?"

Henry replied, "That's fine."

Tom estimated the trip would take two or three hours. Henry was starting to get a little worried, but finally, about three hours after takeoff, Tom and Brooks arrived back home. For some reason, it seemed like Brooks was a little quieter than normal when he and Henry went back to their house. Not much was said about the flight, and when they got home, Ella had supper on the table.

Henry could tell something was on Brooks's mind. He finally came out and asked Brooks, "Son, is there something bothering you?"

Brooks thought for a moment then said, "Mom. Dad. Don't tell him I said this because he asked me not to tell. But on the flight home today…Tom let me fly the plane!"

Henry and Ella looked at each other, then back at Brooks.

"So, did you do something wrong?"

"No. Tom said I did great! I was just afraid that you guys might be mad or something."

Henry thought for a moment, then smiled and said, "Brooks. In my mind, you're a little too young to be flying a plane. But in the almost ten years we've lived here, I've learned that I can trust Tom with just about anything. If he thinks you can fly his plane, then, well I guess it's all right with me."

Brooks let out a huge sigh of relief. "Oh, Mom, Dad, it was fantastic! Just by moving the stick I could make the plane go up or down left or right. It was the most incredible feeling I've ever had. You won't tell Tom I told you, will you?"

Henry laughed, "Brooks, Tom has pretty much become my best friend. I may give him a little grief about it. But your mother and I kind of figured all along that someday you'd be flying planes for Tom. If you're going to learn to fly, well, I would just as soon you learn from Tom and Gene. Just promise me you'll be careful. And don't take any stupid chances."

Brooks was grinning as he replied. "I promise. I'm going to become the best pilot I can possibly be."

Ella said, "That's wonderful dear. Now eat your supper."

Now with his parent's blessing, Brooks's life became an absolute utopia for a teenage boy in the wilds of Kansas. He barely had time for school in between flying lessons, hunting and fishing. Just before his 14th birthday, with Tom seated beside him, Brooks took off and landed the plane by himself. Gene kept kidding Brooks that he was trying to take his job. On rainy days when they couldn't fly, hunt or fish, Brooks would pick the brains of Tom and Gene trying to learn all he could about the art of aviation. Gene would often tell Brooks about flying in World War I and the maneuvers a fighter pilot had to know to stay alive. Gene gave Brooks a vital piece of advice. When a fighter pilot is in a dogfight and he has to make a barrel-roll or a loop, so many times the pilot gets dizzy or disoriented. Don't trust your eyes. See the picture in your inner mind. Trust your instincts, and most of the time you'll be right. Brooks took these words to heart, little knowing that someday they would save his life.

Brooks's flying ability got better and better with

time. By the time he was 16, he was flying solo and began to do crop dusting runs for Tom. Even though Brooks was young, he never allowed the cockiness of youth to cloud his judgment when he was seated in a plane. This was a job, and he knew the trust and faith that Tom, Gene and his parents had in him. Whenever he was in the air, he felt this incredible rush of freedom that he just couldn't experience while on the ground. As a teenager, he couldn't possibly know all the things that life had in store for him. But he felt confident that wherever life took him, a pair of wings would go with him. He was right.

Chapter 10
DRAFTED

It was around that same time that the United States was getting more involved in the war that was brewing. Japan had just bombed Pearl Harbor, and the Americans were ready for war with Germany as well. Not all the news of the world reached a small community in Kansas in a timely fashion. But Henry and Ella were aware of what was happening worldwide, and they prayed that war would end before Brooks became old enough to be drafted.

The town that the Borgmans lived in wasn't large enough to have a high school. So after Graduating from Anomie Grade School, Brooks, along with the other Anomie high schoolers, rode the bus 12 miles to attend high school at Jukesville. The enrollment at Jukesville High was a little over a hundred students. Brooks was near the top of his class academically. His teachers said he could have gotten even higher grades if his mind had been on studies instead of what he was going to do when he got home. One thing that came out during his high school years was Brooks's excellent vision. During a high school physical, the eye doctor said that Brooks's vision was 20/15. That help to explain his good shooting ability as well as his hand to eye coordination. Brooks played basketball and baseball for Jukesville High, and while he was a nice player in both sports, he didn't stand out in either. Primarily, just like academics, his heart wasn't in it. Brooks's focus was on hunting, fishing and flying. Those aren't bad things to be focused on when you're growing up in rural Kansas.

Brooks was a well-liked teenager. He had lots of friends in Anomie and Jukesville. Brooks enjoyed hanging out with a group of friends from time to time, but as far as dating goes, Brooks was always too shy to ask out a girl. Brooks's first date ever was senior prom, and that was actually arranged by mutual friends.

Brooks was in the top ten of his class, grade-wise, when he graduated in May 1944. Brooks had conversations with his parents, as well as Gene, Tom and Reverend Foster, about the war, his duties and his probable draft. It was just before his 19th birthday when he got the letter notifying him that he was being called to duty. This was a hard time for Henry and Ella. They were incredibly proud to call themselves Americans and they knew it was right for their son to do his duty. Yet as any parent would, they just wanted to protect him and keep him safe.

According to the letter, Brooks was to report to Kansas City the week before Thanksgiving. There it would be determined what branch of the military he would be assigned to and where he would do his basic training. Of course with his knowledge of flying, everyone assumed he would be with the Army Air Force.

In the last three weeks he had at home before leaving, Brooks spent most of his time with his mom and dad. They had numerous family talks about a variety of topics, including Henry and Ella's families' histories, as well as the dreams that Henry and Ella had for Brooks's future. Ella, of course, worried about Brooks's safety, but when they were talking she managed to hold back the tears. Henry had the same worries, but he kept them bottled up inside. That last week before he left, Brooks wanted to do a little hunting and fishing, so it was that he and his dad spent a little quality time outdoors.

Coming back from one of those hunting trips, the two Borgman men had time to talk. Henry spoke to his son, "Brooks, there's not a single thing that you could do that would make your mother and me more proud of you than we are right now. In a few months, there's a good chance that you're going to be put in harm's way. Every single American owes this country a debt for allowing us this freedom that we enjoy. If you're called on to fight for that freedom, then I'm telling you to give anything you do your best effort. You owe that to the people around you at the time as well as the people back home that would expect that of you. I'm not asking you to be a hero, just do your job, then come back home to us. In a short while, you and I will be further apart than we've ever been. Just remember…. No matter the distance, there will always be a bridge between your heart and mine. I'll be waiting here to welcome you home when you cross that span again. I love you son."

When Henry had finished, Brooks couldn't find any words to say, so he gave his dad a long hug, then the two of them went into the house to enjoy the supper Ella had prepared.

Chapter 11
BASIC

The day of Brooks's departure had arrived. He was to board the ten o'clock train in Jukesville and travel to Kansas City. He would then find out where he would be heading. Henry and Ella drove Brooks to Jukesville. When they walked up to the train depot, they met Reverend Foster and his wife Hazel, along with Tom and Debbie Shaw and Gene Telford. They had made the trip over to see Brooks off and to support Henry and Ella. There were handshakes and hugs, backslapping and well-wishing, as Brooks prepared to step on the train. He kissed his mom, hugged his dad and picked up his bag and walked to the train car entrance. Just as he was going to place his foot on the step, he felt a tap on his shoulder. He turned around and saw Gene standing there. Gene held out his hand and said, "Here. I want you to take this with you. It's just a little pin with the insignia of our fighter squadron from World War I. It doesn't really mean anything, but we always thought these little pins brought us good luck. It would make me proud to know that you have it with you." Gene turned to walk away then added, "Oh, and you can give it back to me when you come home."

Brooks was choked up but managed to reply, "I'll bring it back to you. Thanks Gene."

Moments later the train was on the roll. The seven folks from Anomie watched until the train was out of sight. Henry and Ella thanked everyone for coming to see Brooks off. The group was fairly quiet as they made their way back to their cars and headed home. For the first time in their lives, the parents and the son were separated. Brooks would certainly miss Mom and Dad, but the exuberance of youth made him anxious to see what lay ahead of him. For Henry and Ella, it would be daily prayers that would help them cope with Brooks's absence. He had only just left and yet they dreamed of the day of his return.

As was expected, Brooks did indeed get assigned to the Army Air Force of the military. He would do his training at Perrin Army Air Force Training Command, Dennison, Texas. The squad he was placed in was mostly young men just like him. For most, it was their first time away from home. They were scared, excited and overwhelmed all at the same time. For the first couple of weeks, it seemed all they did was fill out paperwork, get physicals, do conditioning, and clean their barracks and campgrounds. The man placed in charge of this squad was Sergeant Roker. In the next few months, Brooks became convinced that Sergeant Roker did not possess the ability to smile. It seemed the sergeant yelled at everybody, but Brooks felt he got more than his fair share. Brooks and the sergeant hit it off wrong when in one of their earlier meetings the sergeant asked if anyone had ever been in a plane before. Brooks wanted to impress Sergeant Roker, so he raised his hand and replied that he had been flying planes for several years now. This comment caused the sergeant to believe that Brooks was a braggart and someone in need of being put in their place. Brooks's life in basic training was not going to be easy. Sergeant Roker would see to that.

When they weren't conditioning are cleaning the grounds, the new recruits spent most of their time in classrooms learning about flying. The young men in the squadron were being trained as fighter pilots. Even though Brooks was ahead of his classmates and that he knew how to fly, he would be the first to tell you he was learning a whole lot of things he didn't know. The classes were taught by different instructors, each of who specialized in one or two areas of fighter pilot training. Sergeant Roker didn't actually teach the classes, but he was always there keeping an eye on his squad. It seemed to Brooks like anytime he would look up, Sergeant Roker was staring at him with a scowl on his face. In the evenings when the recruits were back in their barracks, Brooks and the others would talk about learning to fly, life back at their hometowns, the war in general and Sergeant Roker. Every other member of the squad confided in Brooks that it seemed like the sergeant had it in for Brooks. When they would talk about the war in Europe and the Pacific, most of the young men figured they would be sent to the Pacific, because they had heard the war in Europe was winding down. Plus Germany's Air Force was pretty well decimated by the Allied Air Force. No one was in a big hurry to go to battle, but they all agreed they were getting tired of the training in the classrooms. About a week before Christmas, the recruits got their wish of starting to train on real planes. They started off by just sitting in the planes and learning the instrument panels that they had studied in the classroom. The next step was riding with an instructor in the little two-seater recognizance planes. Eventually, the recruits got to fly the planes in the air and later learned to land and take off. Brooks liked the instructor that he had, and he told him that he had been flying crop duster planes for three years now. The instructor watched Brooks handle the plane in the air and was convinced he knew what he was doing. On just a second day with his trainer, Brooks was allowed to take off and land. Upon landing, the instructor told Sergeant Roker that Brooks didn't need any more instruction at this level. They needed to concentrate on the other recruits. Sergeant Roker scowled and sarcastically said, "Well, maybe private Borgman should just teach the class." Brooks was not surprised that he didn't receive a Christmas present from Sergeant Roker.

Brooks did get several gifts from the folks back home. He tried to write a short letter every week letting his mom and dad know how he was doing. By the early part of February, the squad had graduated to getting to fly actual fighter planes. The P-51 Mustang was the most awe-inspiring plane that Brooks had ever seen. Crop-dusting planes turned about three hundred horsepower, these P-51's were almost double that. These fighters that these men would fly were made just to house the pilot. A couple of the training planes had been converted to have a second seat for an instructor to ride along. When it was Brooks's turn, he took off with his instructor seated behind him. The instructor knew that Brooks had already been flying planes, so he asked him, "Do you want to have a little fun?"

Brooks replied, "Okay. What do you mean?"

The instructor continued, "When you go past the viewing grounds were all your buddies are, give them a barrel roll or two and maybe a loop." Brooks twisted around in the cockpit to look at the instructor. They were both smiling.

"You got it," said Brooks. The two barrel rolls and the loop had all the recruits cheering and Sergeant Roker fuming. He felt if one of the other guys tried that, they might get killed.

When Brooks landed, he and the instructor were called over to the bleachers where the rest of the recruits were seated. His classmates started to applaud, but a stern look from Sergeant Roker stopped the applause immediately.

"Well," said Sergeant Roker. "It seems Mr. Borgman here believes he's ready to take on the enemy all by himself. Tomorrow we'll let him show us how to shoot down an enemy plane. Dismissed."

When Roker had left, the instructor told Brooks, "Aw, don't let him get to you kid. You did great."

"But what did the sergeant mean about shooting down an enemy plane?"

The instructor answered, "One of the last tests of a new pilot is to try to shoot up a dummy plane that's being towed by a cable. Tomorrow you'll be by yourself with live ammunition. Don't worry. I know you'll do fine."

Next day, about midmorning, everyone was gathered back at the same place. Brooks had his own real P-51, loaded with ammo. Sergeant Roker told Brooks, "I want you flying at full throttle. You come up from under or over the dummy plane and see if you can hit it. Oh, and Borgman…try not to shoot down the plane that's pulling it."

Brooks was nervous. He knew everyone there was rooting for him...except Roker. Brooks took off and circled to the west as instructed. The transport plane pulling the dummy fighter took off and also circled west. When the dummy plane was nearing the viewing area, Brooks was ordered to make his attack run. Brooks threw the throttle forward and came at his target from underneath. It happened just as Sergeant Roker thought it might. Brooks had never flown this fast before, and he overshot his intended target, almost colliding with the cable towing it.

On this particular test, you only get one try. When Brooks landed, he wanted to hide. He had let down his instructor and his classmates, and he had delighted Sergeant Roker. When he walked up to the grand-stand, Sergeant Roker announced, "Don't feel too bad Borgman. After the other twenty guys get their try, you get to go again."

Brooks had enough. He addressed the sergeant, "Sir. I'd like to try again tomorrow."

Roker replied, "Are you sure your ego can stand another day like today?"

"I know some of what I did wrong. With your per-mission, I'd like to try again tomorrow."

Even though he wouldn't tell Brooks that, Sergeant Roker knew that none of the other recruits were even close to trying this drill. So after a few moments of si-lence, he said, "All right Borgman. You can try again tomorrow. That gives you all night to think up excuses when you fail."

That night in the barracks, Brooks spoke very little to his classmates. He played the scene over and over again in his mind, trying to figure out everything that went wrong. When his buddies had all gone to sleep, Brooks still stared at the dark ceiling, when he sud-denly heard a voice in his head. It was Gene Telford's voice. "Don't trust your eyes. See the picture in your inner mind. Trust your instincts, and most of the time you'll be right."

Brooks sat at the breakfast table the next morning and picked at his food. He just wanted to get in the air. Finally, ten o'clock arrived, and he heard the same speech from Sergeant Roker that he had heard the day before. Brooks took off. The target plane took off.

Brooks was nervous, then he suddenly reached

and felt something in his shirt pocket. It was the pin that Gene had given him at the train station. The nervousness left. A calmness settled over him that he had never felt before. A voice in his radio earpiece said, "Attack." Brooks repeated the maneuver from the day before, only this time he saw everything play out in his mind's eye like the pictures on a movie screen. He pulled up earlier and saw the dummy plane come into site. His guns roared. Pieces flew off the dummy plane as Brooks rocketed past its tail.

On the ground, Sergeant Roker watched the whole thing. He turned to his corporal and said, "When Borgman lands, bring him to my office." With that, he left.

Brooks landed and taxied to a stop. He jogged over to the grandstand as his fellow recruits cheered. The target plane combo landed, and the inspectors examined the dummy plane. The corporal wanted Brooks to leave, but Brooks asked if he could find out his score. The inspectors came before the grandstands and announced that Brooks had put more bullet holes in the dummy plane than any other pilot they had ever tested. Brooks received some handshakes from some of his buddies, then climbed into the corporal's jeep. Brooks was worried about being called to the sergeant's office, and he asked the corporal what this was all about. The corporal answered, "I don't know. He just told me to bring you there. By the way, Borgman that was some really nice flying and shooting you did there."

Brooks replied, "Thanks."

Brooks hopped out of the jeep in front of the sergeant's office, and the corporal drove away. Brooks swallowed hard and took a deep breath as he entered Sergeant Roker's office, all the while wondering what he had done wrong this time.

Brooks opened the door, stepped inside, came to attention, saluted and said, "Private Borgman reporting sir."

Without raising his eyes from the papers he was working on, Sergeant Roker gave a half-hearted salute and said, "At ease. Take a seat, Borgman." Roker continued to write for another minute or so. Finally, he laid down his pen, leaned back in his chair and looked across the desk at Brooks. "Borgman, you did some nice flying out there today."

Brooks was a little taken back with the first complementary words he had ever heard from Sergeant Roker. "Thank you sir."

Roker continued to stare at Brooks for a bit, then spoke, "Borgman, I've been a little tough on you because when you got here, I thought you were a wise-ass that needed to be put in his place." Roker thought for a little more then went on, "My job here is to take a bunch of you mama's boys and in a couple of months get you ready to win a war. It's not my job to be your best friend. I have to make you hate me so much, that you're willing to work extra hard to prove me wrong. Well...today you proved me wrong. When you got here, I saw a cock-sure boy still holding onto some apron strings.... What I saw today was a young man willing to fight to prove to me and to himself, that he was ready to protect his country. Borgman, I'm going to tell you something in confidence. If you tell your friends, I'll deny every word. That person I saw flying that P-51 today, is the best natural pilot I've ever seen come through here. I'm promoting you to active duty. You're shipping out for Europe tomorrow."

Chapter 12
WELCOME TO THE WAR

Brooks was stunned. Both by the kind words from Roker, and the thought of going to war. "Sir, thank you for all that you've done for me. Just one question, sir. I was under the impression that we recruits would be heading for the Pacific."

"You're right. The Pacific does need more fighters. But you're the only one of this group that's ready now. I know you're supposed to be here a few more weeks.… But there is nothing I can teach you that you don't already know. The Nazi Air Force has pretty well been silenced, but the Allies still need some good fighter pilots to help wrap things up over there.

You'll catch a train in the morning and eventually end up in New York. From there they'll ship you to England. You'll get your assignments there. One more thing, You don't ever have to like me, and you never have to send me a Christmas card. But someday, when you're kicking the Nazis' butt, stop and think…Roker would have liked to have seen this. That's all. Good luck son."

Brooks had entered the sergeant's office fully expecting to be chewed out for something. Roker's kind words and praise caught Brooks totally by surprise. Roker's explanation for the way he treated the recruits also started to make sense to Brooks. Brooks's head was swimming with Sergeant Roker's comments as well as the idea that he was heading to England. That evening back at the barracks all the other squad members wanted to know what Roker had told Brooks. Brooks didn't tell the guys all that was said. He simply told them Roker had said he did a good job and he was leaving for England in the morning. All the rest of the recruits wished Brooks good luck and told him to try to stay in touch. When things in the barracks settled down, Brooks wrote his mom and dad a letter, telling them all about what was going on. He ended the letter by telling them he would write again from England.

A couple of days later, Brooks was in New York. He had about a half a day before he had to get on the boat so he made connections with his godfather, Andrew, and spent a couple of hours filling in Andrew all about what had happened since they left New York. Andrew was glad to hear that Henry and Ella were doing well and he was amazed at the man Brooks had turned into. In the restaurant where they were eating, Andrew managed to embarrass Brooks when he stood up and got everyone's attention. "I just wanted you all to know that this young man is my godson. He is leaving for the war in Europe tomorrow. Please keep him in your prayers." A roar went up from the patrons of the restaurant, followed by a round of applause. Many people leaving shook Brooks's hand and wished him good luck. Brooks reported back to the meeting area that evening, and the next morning he was on his way to England. Brooks did not encounter any other pilots on the trip, but he spoke to a lot of young men who were in the infantry. They all hoped the war would be over by the time they got there.

When the boat landed in England, Brooks was taken to the R. A. F. Base at High Wycombe. He was told by his superiors that his destination was yet to be decided. He had a few days to look around London. Other than New York, Brooks had never seen a city the size of London. He bought a few trinkets and packaged them up and had them sent to his mom and dad. One evening, after about a week in England, a sergeant came into Brooks's barracks and told him that he was leaving at o-eight hundred hours the next morning for his assignment. Brooks would be flying on a transport plane filled with supplies for a small airfield in northeastern France. Brooks slept very little that night, as the butterflies in his stomach kept him wondering what lay in store. It turns out the airfield didn't have an official name. It was referred to as A. F. 29. Brooks was the only person on the plane other than the pilot and copilot. As Brooks watched out of the window of the plane, he could see some of the destruction the war had left on the countryside below.

The small towns that the Allies had fought through were pretty much left in ruins. The transport plane landed at A. F. 29, and as Brooks stepped down from the plane, his first impression was that this airstrip had been destroyed. There were bombers and fighter planes that were scattered around the airfield in different stages of ruination. Brooks assumed that the pilots of these aircraft had made it back. But just how some of these things stayed in the air was a mystery to Brooks.

The transport plane had parked on a wide spot on one side of the runway. Presently, Brooks saw a jeep and a truck pull away from some ragtag buildings and head towards the transport. A grubby looking soldier in the jeep and a pair of young men in the truck parked their vehicles and exchanged pleasantries with the transport pilots. The grubby looking guy asked the pilots, "Where's all of our fighter pilots?"

The one pilot pointed at Brooks and said, "You're looking at him Bugs." Bugs looked Brooks up and down, reached out to shake his hand and continued, "No offense kid, but we were expecting a few more pilots to be on this plane. Can you give us a hand off-loading the supplies into the truck?"

"Sure," Brooks replied.

It took about 20 minutes to unload the plane, and shortly after it was empty, it took off, heading back to England. The jeep driver told Brooks to hop in with him. Driving back to the building he said, "My name is Bernard, but everybody calls me Bugs. I'm supposed to be the chief mechanic around here, but I usually end up doing every other job that comes along. What's your name?"

"Well my birth name is Brooklyn Borgman, but everybody calls me Brooks."

"Glad to meet you Brooks. If you don't mind me sayin', you look kinda young. How old are you?"

"I turned nineteen this past October."

Bugs shook his head, "Man. The army's got no business sending you young guys over here. A war is not good for a man at any age, but if the generals had to do all the fighting, this thing would have been over a long time ago." Bugs pulled the jeep up in front of the one building. "Major Stearns runs this place. He's a real nice guy…. Being an officer and all. Come on in…. I'll introduce you."

Brooks followed Bugs into the major's office. Bugs spoke to the major. "Major, this is the only pilot that was on the plane. Must be that all the other Allied pilots are on vacation in England this week. This is Brooks Borgman."

Brooks stood at attention and saluted his new commanding officer. Major Stearns stood up and returned the salute. "Brooks, I'm glad you're with us but I gotta tell you, the Army didn't do you any favors sending you here."

"How's that sir?" asked Brooks.

"Well, we're about the closest airfield to the front lines. We seem to get some of the nastiest assignments. I suppose you saw the plane graveyard outside?"

"I did notice a lot of wrecked planes."

"Most of the pilots got their planes back there, but

often times they were too shot up to put back in the air. Bugs keeps pullin' parts off of those planes trying to keep our few remaining planes flying. Right now we've got one B-17 bomber available and four P-51 fighters. Besides yourself, we've only got two other fighter pilots on the base right now."

Bugs broke in, "If you call those two pilots. I call them something else."

Major Stearns kind of nodded in agreement to Bugs statement. "The two pilots Bugs is referring to are named Dunning and Devlin. I'm not really sure which side they're on in this war. Whenever they get sent out on a mission, they always return with their planes unscathed. Their ammunition is usually gone, but our other troops never report ever seeing those two where they're supposed to be. Take my advice son. Stay away from them two as much as you can. And don't ever trust your life with them."

Bugs added, "I say we give them to the Germans."

Brooks asked the major, "What kind of missions do you fly out of here?"

"Well Brooks, nowadays, we mostly just fly support for our ground troops. We try to give them a hand while they're trying to push that front-line back to Berlin. It's different from the first part of the war. We don't encounter that many enemy fighters anymore. Most of the damage to our planes are from artillery and ground fire."

Just then the door opened, and a half-dozen men joined them in Major Stearns office. The major said, "Andy, I'm glad you're here. Let me introduce you to

Brooks Borgman, a new fighter pilot. Brooks, this is the crew of our B–17 bomber. This is the crew leader, Lieutenant Andy Garbs. This is co-pilot Seth O'Brien and the gunners and the rest of the crew, Kelly, Kirby, Sullivan and Davis. You met Richards and Thompson. They're out unloading the truck. Brooks, I advise you to spend all your spare time with these guys or Bugs. They are some of the nicest guys and some of the best soldiers that the allies have available."

Lieutenant Garbs spoke for the crew, "Thank you, Major. Brooks, welcome to our little slice of heaven. I suppose the major told you about the other two pilots we have here?"

Brooks answered, "Yes sir. I'm looking forward to getting to know all you guys."

Major Stearns spoke again, "Bugs you show Brooks where his bunk is, then take him to the mess hall to get something to eat. Spend the afternoon getting to know the place and the rest of these guys. Andy, how about tomorrow, you and Brooks take two of the fighters out for a reconnaissance run. It'll give Brooks a chance to see the area around here."

"You got it," replied Lieutenant Garbs.

Bugs grabbed Brooks's arm, "Now we're going to the most dangerous spot in the war. The mess hall."

Everyone had smiles as they left Major Stearns's office.

Chapter 13
THE MISSION

The next morning after breakfast Lieutenant Garbs and Brooks headed for the airstrip. When they passed the B–17 bomber, Brooks looked up and saw a name written on the nose of the plane.

He spoke the name out loud, "Ruby Sinclair." He looked back at Lieutenant Garbs and asked, "Who's that?"

Andy bowed his head and smiled. "Well, that's actually my mother's maiden name. My dad died when I was young, and my mother raised me by herself. When I got assigned as commander of this plane, they told me I could name it whatever I wanted. I didn't want to put the name Garbs up there because people would think I'm trying to blow my own horn. So I used her maiden name. I reasoned that no one protected me better in my young life than mom, so I thought maybe that name would help this plane protect me now." Andy looked at Brooks and smiled, "It's worked so far."

"That's a great idea," said Brooks.

Lieutenant Garbs continued, "When you get your plane, you can call it whatever you want. You don't have to use a person's name. Just call it something that gives you happy memories of home."

With that Lieutenant Garbs and Brooks were at the airstrip. They climbed in and fired up a couple of P-51's and took to the sky. Major Stearns did indeed want Brooks to see some of the countryside, but he also wanted Lieutenant Garbs to kind of evaluate the new pilot. They flew for almost 2 hours with no encounters with the Germans. They landed back at A. F. 29 and Bugs met them there to service the two planes. Lieutenant Garbs told Brooks to head back to the barracks. He had to talk to Major Stearns. Andy told the major, "Brooks handled that plane like a ten-year veteran. I think we got ourselves a good pilot there."

"That's good to hear Andy. I'd feel even better if we never had to use him."

Brooks would be put to use sooner than anyone could know. That evening, as everyone was preparing for bed, Bugs came banging on the barracks' door. "Something big just came over the radio! Everybody report to the major's office immediately!" The B-17 crew along with Brooks, Devlin and Dunning all hustled to Major Stearns's office.

The major asked everyone to take a seat. The look on his face told the group this was not business as usual.

"I just got a call from Allied command in England.

As you know, Germany's losing the war. But Hitler has decided to try to bust through the lines and lengthen this thing out longer. It seems that the underground has just found out that Germany's pulling a whole division of tanks from the Russian front and sending them through the mountains to try to break through the Allied front in northern Germany. The Allied commanders are convinced if those tanks make it there, we can't hold the line. If they break through, it could cause chaos, not to mention costing us thousands of more lives and extending the war for months."

"How do we fit in here, Major?" Lieutenant Garbs asked.

"There's only one bridge those tanks can use to get out of the mountains. It's at Ugarde. If that bridge could be blown, the tanks will never arrive."

Sergeant O'Brien asked, "Can't England just send some bombers over there to knock out that bridge?"

"We just got this information. The tanks will be there tomorrow morning. The only bomber close enough to reach that bridge before the tanks…is ours."

Lieutenant Garbs spoke, "Sir. By the time we could reach that bridge it will be daylight. It would be suicide."

Major Stearns sat down in his chair and covered his face with his hands, "I know that Andy." After a few moments of silence, he continued, "Allied command knows that too. But if we could somehow miraculously knock out that bridge, the German tanks will be out of the picture. The thought of cutting six months off the war and saving thousands of lives…makes England believe that the lives of one bomber crew are worth the risk. They are ordering you to make a run at that bridge."

"The Germans know that bridge is vital, so they've surrounded it with ground troops. The underground can't get close. The only chance of destroying it is through the air. You guys leave at 0200 hrs. I only wish I could send some fighters to help you…. But it's out of their fuel range."

Brooks raised his hand, "Sir. If the fighters could go with them, would it help?"

Major Stearns said, "If we could have fighter cover…. Well, we might just make it. But it's just not possible."

Brooks spoke again, "Sir, what if instead of a bomb underneath our P-51's, we strapped a 50-gallon drum full of gas. We would rip out some auxiliary fuel switches from those wrecked bombers around here and mount them in the fighters. We run a plastic hose into the drums and run our fighters off that fuel first. When the drum goes empty, we switch to our regular tanks and drop the drums away. It would buy us two more hours of flying time."

Private Dunning leaned toward Brooks and softly said, "What's a matter kid? You in a hurry to die?"

Brooks went on, "We'll tie a little weight on to the plastic hose, say like a half-inch wrench so that the hose stays at the bottom of the drum to get the maximum amount of fuel available. That extra drum of fuel would give the fighters almost as much range as the bomber."

Major Stearns's eyes opened wider as he listened

to the ideas coming out of this young man's head. He turned to Bugs and asked, "Can you do that? And can you do that in time?"

Bugs was just as wide-eyed as the major as he listened to Brooks's ideas. He then turned to the major and said, "Yah. I think that could work."

Major Stearns told Bugs, "If you can pull that off, then the fighters will go with Lieutenant Garbs." He then looked at Brooks, "Son, I thank you for your ideas but I don't know if you understand the difficulty of this mission. Even if you could protect the bomber to the bridge, you won't have enough fuel to make it back."

Brooks responded, "Sir, I'm just thinking of the bomber crew. If we can help them pull this off...well isn't that what we're supposed to do?"

"Yah Brooks.... It is. Andy, you guys, won't have enough fuel to make it back either. If you make it to the bridge and drop your load, turn towards Norway and try to get as far as you can. Hopefully, the underground can find you and get you back to England. As for you fighter pilots, you turn north as well. If you run out of fuel, bail out. Best case scenario, you spend a few months in a prisoner of war camp, and then you get rescued and go home. Okay everyone, listen up. Allied command knows how important this mission could be. They told me to tell you, anyone going on this mission and getting back...gets an automatic honorable discharge from service.... You get to go home."

Devlin sneers, "The discharge won't do us much good if we're dead."

Sergeant O'Brien glared back at Devlin and Dunning. "You guys haven't done much good while you're alive!"

Major Stearns calls out, "That's enough! We don't have much time. Kelly, Kirby, Borgman. You help Bugs rig up the drums on the fighters. The rest of you guys make sure the B-17 is ready to go. Andy. You and Seth go over the flight plan to get you to that bridge. Everybody get going."

Brooks and the other three grabbed flashlights and headed out the door. Bugs turned to Brooks and said, "That's a great idea kid. You seem to have the plan in your head. Tell us what to do."

"Well," said Brooks, "Bugs why don't you go through those wrecked bombers and try to find three fuel tank switches. Kirby can go to the supply hut and get about 30 feet of fuel hose, some hose clamps, some little wrenches or weights of some kind, about six ratchet straps and some wire. Kelly and I will get three fuel drums and three wooden fence posts." The list sounded kind of confusing to the others but everyone left in a hurry to get the things that Brooks wanted.

When they met back at the planes, Bugs asks Brooks, "What's the fence post for?"

"Well, that clamp under the plane that normally carries a little bomb is about the diameter of a fence post. We'll fasten the post to the bomb release clamp, hold the barrel up under the fence post and attach it to the post with a ratchet strap on each end of the barrel. Make sure that the little hole in the barrel is pointed up. We then tie our weight onto the end of the fuel hose using some wire. Feed about two or three feet of the hose into the barrel. Bugs, you go into the cockpit of each plane and splice that fuel splitter valve into the existing fuel line. We'll run this new line up into the cockpit, and you can attach it to the splitter valve. When all that is in place, we need to fill the tanks with gas and siphon the gas up to the valve. If this works and the plane runs on that gas from the drum first, then the drum should go empty in about two hours. When it does, you switch to your regular fuel tanks, pull the plastic hose off the valve and hit the bomb release. The drum, the fence post and the plastic hose should all just fall away."

Bugs shook his head in amazement, "I sure hope we all survived this war. Cause if we do, I'm going into business with you kid."

The four men worked fast trying to retrofit the P-51s. The project actually worked very well. Brooks's plane was the last completed, and when they step back to admire their work, Bugs swung his flashlight across the engine cover of Brooks's plane. "What's that writing on your plane?"

"Well," said Brooks a little embarrassed. "Everybody seems to have their plane named after a girl or something special. I named mine after something that makes me think of home."

Bugs put the flashlight beam on the words again and read out loud, "Cherry Pie."

Brooks responded, "I know that probably sounds silly to you guys, but it brings back special memories for me."

"Make sense to me kid. I can't think of too much

more that would remind me of home than cherry pie. Good name."

The four men hustled back to Major Stearns's office to tell him the long-range fighters were ready to go.

With 15 minutes till takeoff time, the mood in Major Stearns's office was somber, to say the least. The major ran through the plan again. No one else spoke. After a few moments of silence the major said, "As I told you guys before, it troubles my heart to send you out on a mission this dangerous. If there was anything else, I could do...I would. I repeat—bailing out and spending the rest of the war in a prison camp is not the end of the world. Do your best.... But you don't have to die trying to do your best. Grab your gear and hit your planes."

Bugs was busy helping the bomber crew get in their plane. When they were all on board, he swung his flashlight beam around and saw Brooks caring a little satchel on his way to his fighter. "What's in the bag?" asked Bugs.

"Oh, just some supplies," replied Brooks. "Back home we never went in the air without extra engine oil, hose clamps, line patches, electric tape and a few tools. I guess it might be silly...but I just feel better if I got the stuff with me."

"It don't sound silly to me," answered Bugs. "Kid, I gotta tell you something." Bugs put his hands on Brooks's shoulders and looked him in the eyes. "I realize I've only known you for a couple of days, but I feel there's something special about you. I know this runs going to be tough, but I feel like you might be our good luck charm. I'll be looking forward to seeing you when you get back."

Brooks stepped forward and he and Bugs hugged. With that, he turned and climbed into his plane.

A few moments later Brooks heard Lieutenant Garbs tell Bugs to turn on the lights at the edges of the runway. They weren't very bright, but at least you could see where the runway was supposed to be. All the planes had their engines running. The B-17 headed out first, followed by the three fighters. All the pilots were told to keep radio silence, but they could talk from plane to plane on their intercoms. Apparently, every man was alone with their thoughts as the four Allied aircraft flew along in the early morning darkness. Brooks was pleased that his idea for the fuel drums seemed to be working. They were approaching two hours in the air when Brooks's plane started to sputter. He called on the intercom and informed Lieutenant Garbs that his drum had run out of fuel. He was switching to his regular tanks. He started to lose elevation as his Rolls-Royce engine in his P-51 fought through the air bubbles in the fuel line. After ten or fifteen seconds it started to run smoothly again, and a smile broke out on Brooks's face in the darkness of his cockpit.

Time to lose the drum was Brooks's thought. He pulled the fuel line off the splitter valve and hit his bomb release. Everything went according to plan as the fence post, drum and fuel line headed for the German landscape below.

Only a minute or two later, Devlin and Dunning

told Lieutenant Garbs that they had also jettisoned their fuel drums, but now their planes weren't running properly. "I think we'll have to turn back" was their message to the lieutenant.

Lieutenant Garbs had assumed all along with these two would pull something. "Listen you two. Your planes are running just fine. Stay on your course!"

There was a chuckle in Dunning's voice when he told Garbs, "Sorry we can't go with you Lieutenant… but we're turning back."

Lieutenant Garbs was almost yelling when he replied, "I'm ordering you two to stay with the mission. If you turn back. I'll see both of you court-martialed!"

Dunning laughed out loud into his microphone as he told the lieutenant, "It's kinda hard to court-martial us when you're dead. Goodbye Lieutenant."

After a minute of silence, Lieutenant Garbs was a little calmer when he came back on the headset, "Borgman, why don't you turn back as well. I know you're willing to stay with us, but I don't know what one fighter can do anyway. Just go back and tell Major Stearns I want Devlin and Dunning court-martialed for disobeying orders."

Brooks didn't take long to respond, "Sir…if you don't mind, I'd really like to go with you and see if I can help. Please, sir."

"Yah Borgman…. That's okay…. Thanks.!"

What could one fighter do? More than any of this group could have imagined. Brooks possessed more flying skills than even he could realize. Those skills would be put to the ultimate test in a very short while.

Nothing more was spoken on the headsets. In the belly of the B-17, five members of the crew were gathered together talking. They had heard the conversations between Lieutenant Garbs and the fighter pilots. Kelly said, "Wow, that Brooklyn kid is too nice for his own good."

Kirby asked back, "What do ya mean, Brooklyn?"

"That's his real name. He was born on the Brooklyn Bridge. Bugs told me so. Everybody just calls him Brooks."

"I didn't know that."

When a pink glow started to appear in the eastern sky, Brooks called to Lieutenant Garbs, "Sir. If it's okay with you, I'm going to drop back a little ways and maybe climb another thousand feet or so. If we do run into any German fighters, that will give me a nice vantage point to make a run at them. I'm pretty sure they won't be expecting you to have any fighter coverage this deep in Germany."

"Yah Borgman. That's good thinking…. And Borgman…good luck."

"Good luck to you sir."

Brooks took his position. His heart was pounding as his eyes darted back and forth, searching for possible enemy planes. All the gunners on the B-17 were at their posts. They didn't have long to wait. Mike Davis, the tail gunner, saw them first. In the intercom, he shouted, "Here they come! Five of them coming from behind."

The Messerschmitt 109 pilots must have felt like they had been given a present. A lone American bomber this deep in Germany. They were probably argu-ing which one would shoot it down. They lined up to make a pass at the B- 17. On the bomber, the gun-ners gripped their weapons as beads of perspiration built on their foreheads. Just as the men of the B-17 were sure the Germans would start their attack, ma-chine-gun fire filled the air. Brooks had come swoop-ing in at full speed lining up the row of German planes in order to take full advantage of his surprise first pass. Brooks's aim with his P-51 was just as accurate as his little 22 rifle back home.

Two of the German pilots never knew what hit them. The canopy glass on their cockpits exploded as Brooks's bullets sent two planes to the earth below.

"Holy crap!" yelled Davis. "Borgman took out two of them on his first pass!"

Now the dogfight was on. Brooks no longer had the element of surprise on his side. After his initial pass, Brooks rolled back behind the remaining three Messerschmitts. The German pilots broke formation as everyone was now trying to get Brooks in their sites. Every time the German planes came close enough, the B-17 gunners cut loose with their own fire. After a few minutes, it was evident that one German pilot decid-ed to attack the B-17. Brooks saw him break out of the dogfight and Brooks poured the coals to his Rolls-Royce engine. He came at the German from under-neath...just as he had done on that dummy plane back in Texas. When Brooks's machine-gun barked, a third German plane headed for dirt.

Side gunner Kelly yelled in his microphone, "Hell

Lieutenant, Borgman's got the whole German Air Force tied up by himself. I don't think he needs us."

Even though the German pilots were fighting for their lives, they had to know that their main mission was to knock down the bomber. Another German fighter broke away and headed for the B-17. Brooks took out after him. The Messerschmitt and the B-17 gunners were trading fire when Brooks got the German fighter in his sights. He recorded kill number four on his first mission of the war. But this one came at a price. While Brooks was chasing German number four, number five was chasing Brooks. Just after Brooks KO'd his fourth German plane, he felt his P-51 get rocked by bullets. Brooks's flight path took him past Kelly's side gun on the B-17. With the last German fighter concentrating on Brooks, he didn't realize he was in range of Kelly's machine guns. Kelly silenced the last of the German planes. Brooks was unhurt physically, but the smoke was beginning to pour into his cockpit. He scanned his instrument panel and saw that his oil pressure gauge read zero. Just as he would have done back home with one of Tom Shaw's planes, he instinctively shut off his engine.

He called out to the B-17, "Lieutenant Garbs, I've lost oil pressure. I imagine a bullet hit an oil line. I've shut off my engine to keep it from locking up. I'm gonna glide this thing down and see if I can land someplace. If it's something I can fix, I'll try to catch up with you."

Lieutenant Garbs replied, "Son, you've already done more than I would have ever thought possible.

Just on the chance that you get that thing going again, you high-tail it for home. Brooks…you've given us… and this mission a chance…. Thank you."

In the belly of the B-17, Kelly slumped down in the seat next to his machine-gun. He looked across the plane at Kirby, "Oh my God! Have you ever seen anyone fly a plane like that? Most guys couldn't hit the ocean traveling that fast! He was dead on the money on all four of those Germans' I can't believe it!"

Lieutenant Garbs came on the headsets, "Everybody keep your eyes open. We're less than forty minutes from the bridge."

As Brooks was silently letting his plane guide to the earth, he spotted a roadway that he could possibly land on. He couldn't see any power poles next to the road, so he aimed to set the P-51 down there. The road was a little bumpy, but the landing went fine. Brooks jumped out onto the wing and open the shield covering the extremely hot engine. You could say that Brooks was lucky or unlucky, depending on your point of view. He no sooner opened the cover when he saw the problem.

A bullet had indeed nicked in oil line that led to the oil filter. It was repairable. Brooks grabbed his bag from behind his seat. He fashioned a quick patch over the hole and secured it with three hose clamps. He wrapped the whole splice with electric tape and poured in the quarts of oil he had brought along. He was sure the engine would not get full of oil, but it might be enough to keep it running. He closed the shield and reached for his bag just as he heard voices yelling in the distance. He looked up to see German ground troops running his way. He heard the sounds of rifle fire as he threw his bag behind the seat and scrambled back into the cockpit. He silently said a little prayer as he hit the start button. The engine roared to life. Brooks threw the throttle forward as he watched the oil pressure gauge. Fifty yards down the road the needle jumped off the zero. A few moments later, Brooks was in the air. Brooks didn't obey Lieutenant Garb's order to head back. Instead, he raced as fast as he could in the direction of the bridge. He knew the coordinates that the bomber was heading for and he hoped he could catch up. In case they needed him. They would need him. Brooks assumed that the B–17 would stay at about the same elevation it had been traveling so he climbed back to a thousand feet higher as he did before. The bomber crew nervously scanned the sky watching for more trouble. They were now less than 30 minutes from their target. Copilot O'Brien was the first to spot another wave of German fighters. He yelled in his headset, "Bandits at nine o'clock!"

Everyone swung their eyes to the rear of the B-17. Kirby, the other side gunner, spoke out loud to no one in particular, "No! No! No! You can't let us get this close and lose out now! Somebody help us!" He didn't know it then but that somebody was a 19-year-old kid from Kansas.

The situation was almost the same as before. Five more Messerschmitt's were going to try to keep the B-17 from reaching its destination. Also just like before, the fighters lined up as they readied for an attack run. And just like before, the crew of the B-17 and the German fighters were surprised when machine-gun fire was followed by an olive-drab streak rocketing past the rear of the bomber. Brooks was back in the war…and two German planes weren't.

Mike Davis yelled from his tail gun position, "Yahoo! The kid is back."

Kirby rolled his eyes upward and said, "Thank you."

Lieutenant Garbs wanted to yell at Brooks for not heading back, but he knew that Brooks just might make the difference in whether they reach the bridge or not. The dogfight was just like the last one. The Germans were confused over the American pilot this deep in Germany. Brooks was darting and diving quicker than the Germans could follow with their sights. Machine guns were rattling from the fighters as well as the B-17. Brooks took out a third plane in this fight and Davis sent another to the ground. Only one Messerschmitt left. This German fighter was intent on taking out Brooks. And Brooks had a problem.… He was out of ammo. Something told Brooks, if he made a run for it, the German might follow. But what if he didn't. One fighter could still down the B-17. Brooks also knew that they were very close to their target. If this German fighter was gone…the Germans probably couldn't scramble any more planes before the bridge would be wiped out. Brooks heard his father's voice say, "Always do your best." Brooks became the fox.… The German was the hound. Brooks eased back on the throttle so the German could catch up. The kid from Kansas swung his plane around so he could fly past the left side of the B-17.

In his headset, Brooks called out, "Kelly, I'm out of ammo! I'm going to lead him past you!"

Everyone on the B-17 seemed to scream out at the same time, "No! Don't do it!"

Lieutenant Garbs yelled, "Borgman, take evasive action! Do not make yourself a target! I repeat, do not make yourself a target!"

In the belly of the plane, Kirby jumped over to look out Kelly's window, "Kill him Kelly! Kill him! Kill him now!"

In the one or two seconds after Lieutenant Garbs'order, machine guns roared from both the German fighter and the B-17.... Both fighters went down. Everyone on the bomber tried to find a place to look out of as they watched Brooks and the Cherry Pie tumble toward earth. A trail of black smoke followed Brooks as he went out of sight. The crew of the B-17 was in shock. This naïve young kid that they hardly knew, on one mission, had proved to be the best fighter pilot they had ever seen. Then he more or less sacrificed himself for the sake of the mission. They were still alive because of Brooklyn Borgman. Bombardier Richards broke the silence. "Guys. The bridge is in range in less than five minutes."

In the cockpit, Lieutenant Garbs used his sleeve to wipe his eyes. He cleared his throat best he could and said, "Richards...you got the plane. Unload when you're ready.... And Bob...don't miss. The cost of this bridge just got a hell of a lot higher."

At the bridge, the German ground troops had been cheering as they watched the Tiger tanks descending down the mountain road. Their cheers were silenced when they heard the drone of an approaching plane. The troops began running from the bridge.

Bombardier Richards trusted his instruments. When they said now, he hit the bomb release.

As soon as the bombs were away, Garbs swung his plane northward. Everyone on the plane tried to keep an eye on the bridge. Richard's aim was true. The superstructure of the bridge rocked and shook as each of the bombs found their mark. Mixed with the deafening sounds of the bombs exploding was the crashing sound of steel. When the smoke cleared, the remains of the bridge rested in the bottom of the ravine. The Germans were in shock. The ground troops stared in disbelief at the twisted metal lying in the river below. The tank commanders were likewise in shock. How did one lone Allied bomber get this deep in German territory? Their spirits were crushed…as was their mission.

On the B-17, a subdued cheer rang out over the unexpected success of this mission. The cheer quickly faded, and the crew once again drifted away in silent thought at the price that was paid for the completion of the mission. Four of the crew were gathered in the hull of the plane when Kirby said, "I hope that no-name bridge was worth it."

Kelly stared at the floor for a few more seconds then looked up. "That's not a no-name bridge…. It's Brooklyn's bridge."

Kirby gave a little laugh and nodded his head, "Yah.... Brooklyn's Bridge."

Lieutenant Garbs came on the headset, "Everybody keep your eyes peeled. I doubt the Germans are in a fighting mood right now, but you never know. I have no idea if and when we cross the Norway border, but whenever this thing runs out of fuel we'll have to put her down or bailout."

The last hour in the air was uneventful for the B-17. Garbs felt sure they had crossed over into Norway, but he really didn't know. Number one engine began to sputter. Garbs shut down engines one and four to save the fuel for engines two and three. It seemed like the landscape below was nothing but trees. There was no place to land, and it was dangerous to bailout. Engine number two began to cough. In the distance, Lieutenant Garbs saw a clearing. It appeared to be a meadow, and it might be big enough to land the B-17.

He told O'Brien, "Throw down the landing gear. Everybody back there hang on!"

By the time the landing gear was down, engine number two had stopped. Number three was the only prop that was still spinning. Then it quit also. The plane and its crew were now committed to trying to land. They were too low to bail out. Garbs and O'Brien were trying to hold the nose up until they cleared the last of the trees. The tires of the plane knocked off some leaves as the shadow of the B-17 now could be seen on the meadow grass. One bounce, then two.... Then the plane stayed down, speeding along through the sheep pasture. Garbs and O'Brien threw all they had into applying the brakes. She came to a stop just as she reached the far trees. Everyone was ecstatic to be alive and back on the ground, but there was no time to celebrate just yet. As garbs and O'Brien came out of the cockpit, the Lieutenant yelled, "Everyone grab your side arms and get out of the plane and into those trees."

In less than a minute everyone was crouched behind Lieutenant Garbs in the trees. He told the men, "We need to get away from this plane, but I'm not sure what direction to go."

Kirby pointed out towards the meadow, "Why don't we ask those guys?"

Four apparent civilians were running towards the crew. One of them started yelling, "Americans. Over here. Americans. Over here."

Lieutenant Garbs stood up and stepped out of the trees, but he kept his pistol ready.

The four men ran up to him, and the one shook his hand. "Americans. We are with the underground. Come with us."

Lieutenant Garbs asked back, "How do we know this isn't a trap?"

The man shrugged his shoulders, "I guess you don't. But you have to trust someone. We all hate the Germans. Please let us help you."

Garbs motioned to the rest of the crew, "Let's go."

They followed the four men for about a mile to a quaint-looking farmstead. They cautiously followed the men into the house. Several women were inside, and they graciously greeted the Allied flight crew.

"Come sit down at the table. We'll get you something to eat."

The man who had been doing the talking slapped Lieutenant Garbs on the back and said, "This is so wonderful. You flew a mission into Germany, and you all made it safely back here!"

Deep in thought, Lieutenant Garbs stared out the window and solemnly replied, "Yah.... All but one."

Chapter 14
STAYING ALIVE

The crew of the B-17 couldn't have known it, but the one that Garbs was talking about was still alive. When the German fighter pilot riddled Brooks's plane, Brooks did suffer severe injuries. Bullets or shrapnel pierced Brooks's right shoulder, rib cage and thigh. Upon being hit, Brooks immediately passed out. When he came to, his whole body screamed with pain. Brooks was trying to mentally grasp what was going on. His plane was spinning around and around as it plummeted toward the earth and he knew he had to try to get it under control quickly. When he instinctively reached for the stick with his right hand, he felt pain like nothing he had ever known before. He looked at himself and saw his bloody right shoulder and thigh. Through the pain, he grabbed the stick with his left hand and pulled back hard. He managed to get it back under control, but when he looked ahead, he saw the ground rapidly coming to meet him. He continued to put all his strength into leveling out the P-51. With mere seconds to spare, the plane became parallel with the ground. Brooks knew that the plane's belly was about to hit the dirt and he had no choice on selecting a landing site.

The impact of hitting the ground caused the pain level in Brooks's body to skyrocket once again. Brooks had somehow been fortunate enough to have his plane come down on a gravel road that led to a small farm just outside a little village. Rocks and metal careened from the plane's underside at as it skidded toward an old barn. The wings were knocked off as the fuselage disappeared into the heart of the barn and came to a stop. Even though he was somewhat disoriented, Brooks knew immediately he had to get out of that plane. With his left hand, he undid his harness and slid back the cockpit canopy. Through sheer will, and his left arm and leg, Brooks flipped out of the cockpit and landed on his back on the plane's wing. It would have been so easy just to lay there and give up, but through the excruciating pain, he could hear his father's voice urging him to keep fighting.

Brooks managed to stand himself up by leaning against the hull of the P-51. Brooks looked around. His plane was on fire, and the barn soon would be. He had to get out. When he looked out the hole in the barn that his plane had made, he saw a man running towards him carrying a rifle. Though he wasn't in uniform, Brooks figured it had to be a German soldier.

Brooks wore a 45 caliber pistol on his right side, but his right arm wouldn't allow him to retrieve it from the holster. With his left hand, Brooks grabbed his belt and managed to twist the holster out in front of him. He drew the sidearm and turned to see the German bringing his rifle to aim. Brooks fired first. All that target practice back home came into play. The German dropped dead to the ground. The hayloft of the barn was now in flames as Brooks's mind whirled, trying to decide a course of action.

Brooks figured if the Germans were to examine the wreckage of the plane and not find the pilot's body, they would continue to look for him and Brooks was in no shape to run. He settled on a plan. He holstered his pistol and hobbled to the dead German. He tossed the rifle into the flames and grabbed the collar of the dead man's shirt. Working with one arm, one leg and a whole lot of adrenaline, Brooks was able to drag the German close to the plane. The German was indeed wearing dog tags. Brooks ripped them off and tossed them away. He then removed his own dog tags and slipped them over the man's head. Brooks assumed the fire would destroy the man's identity and the dog tags might make the Germans believe that he was the pilot. Brooks saw some daylight coming through the back corner of the barn. He worked his way there and crawled through a hole to escape the burning structure.

Brooks found himself in chest-high weeds and saw trees about fifty yards to the north of the barn. He willed himself to try to get to those trees. About halfway there, he heard the barn collapse behind him.

Once in the trees, he noticed the lay of the land sloped down towards a small river about forty yards distant. His body felt like it was on fire from the constant pain. He had to get to the cool water. He stumbled and fell a couple of times as he worked his way towards the river. Finally, at the water's edge, he could see that it was a clear running stream that appeared to be a foot or two deep. He unhitched his belt and allowed himself to slip into the water. The coolness of the river felt so good as it enveloped his wounds. Brooks laid his head on the gravel bank and passed out. A half an hour or so went by when Brooks awakened shivering in the cool water. He raised his head and checked for soldiers that might be near. Seeing none, he crawled up on the riverbank. For the first time, Brooks tried to see his injuries and check their severity. The hole in his shoulder and the cut on his side, he assumed were from flying metal. There was a round entrance and exit hole on his thigh, leading him to diagnose that a bullet had done the damage there. The cool water had helped to clean the wounds and slow up the bleeding.

Brooks took out the sulfa powder in his belt pouch and did the best he could applying it to his wounds. It was a fairly warm day, and Brooks knew he must try to hide while it was light. With his one good arm, he raked together a large pile of leaves and dead grass. He then did his best to burrow into his nest. He hoped the leaves would conceal him as well as help warm him back up. Going into the river was the right thing to do at the time, but now he desperately needed some heat to avoid hypothermia. His body still ached as he settled into his hiding spot. His mind was a whirl with thoughts of everything that happened in the past few days. Tears of emotion welled up inside him as he thought about his dad and mom, and how the news of him being shot down would devastate not only them but the whole town that he loved. Thankfully, he fell asleep.

When Brooks awoke, it was nighttime. He figured if he was going to try to move it had to be now. He found a tree limb to use as a crutch. Even through all the pain, he started to move westward through the timber. He wanted to try to get away from the barn in case the dog tags didn't fool the Germans. He could only make fifty to a hundred yards each time before he had to stop to rest. He moved off and on through the night and by the time daylight started to appear Brooks was totally exhausted. He once again covered himself up with leaves and fell asleep. About mid-day he was awakened by yelling voices. He rose up on his knees and peered in that direction. It turned out he was not far from the edge of the small town.

A German major and two soldiers were dragging an older man and a young woman from a nearby house. Thanks to the lessons his mother had taught him, Brooks understood the German language as he listened to the major accuse the man of being a spy. The man was the young lady's father, and she was scream-ing for the Germans to let him go. The major drew his Luger pistol and smiled evilly as he fired three bullets into the woman's father. The woman was crying and screaming as the major grabbed her by her hair. The major smiled at the other two soldiers and told them they could leave, but he was going take the girl into the woods and thoroughly interrogate her. The soldiers nodded and laughed. The major drug the girl, heading in the direction where Brooks was concealed. Once in the woods, the major told the young lady to disrobe. Through her tears, the girl spit in the face of the German major. The major hit her hard on the cheek, knocking her to the ground.

The young lady was dazed as the major knelt down between her legs. The young lady opened up her eyes and saw the major laughing down at her. As the major reached for the top button her of her blouse, his eyes suddenly popped wide-open, and the major cried out with a fairly loud "AAWGH!" Then, he collapsed on the ground next to the young lady. Brooks had snuck up behind the German and stabbed him with his knife. The other two German soldiers were just getting into their truck when they heard the major cry out. They looked at one another, then smiled. One of them said, "It sounds like the interrogation is going well."

They laughed and then drove off. Brooks put his finger to his lips, motioning for the woman to be quiet. He helped her up and softly spoke to her in German asking if she was all right. She nodded yes, then in English asked Brooks, "Are you an American?" Brooks was surprised she knew English and he replied that he was the American pilot who crashed his plane the day before a mile or so away. The woman said she had heard that the pilot was dead. Brooks told her he had switched dog-tags with a dead man to try to fool the Germans.

Suddenly the woman remembered her murdered

father. "Papa," she cried out. She turned and was going to run to him.

Brooks grabbed her arm. "Please don't go. There's nothing you can do and if the Germans see you, they will kill you too. We need to hide." The woman wiped the tears from her cheeks and nodded in agreement. Brooks asked her if she could help drag the German major's body down to the river and throw it in. She nodded yes and then notice for the first time that Brooks was badly hurt.

She said, "I'm so sorry…. I failed to notice your injuries. Can I help you?"

Brooks said, "I'll be all right for the moment. Let's get rid of the dead German and then hide out until dark."

She agreed. They dumped the body in the river and then hid in the brush as they waited for nightfall.

While hiding in the brush, the two began to talk.

Brooks introduced himself. The girl's name was Ellen Miden. Brooks asked her how she had come to speak English so well. She explained that she lived with her aunt in New York City while going to high school there. She was planning to go to college to become a nurse. But when the war got bad in Germany, she came back to try to get her parents out. When she got to Germany, she found out her mother had been killed by the Nazis. Her father was helping the Allied underground and was a wanted man. The Nazis found Ellen and her father today right before Brooks saw him get murdered. Ellen's father's name was Herman, and it was, in fact, he who had notified the allies about the German tank movement. The very mission on which Brooks was shot down. Brooks told Ellen that he was born in New York on the Brooklyn Bridge. That's how he got his name. He told her his family moved to Anomie, Kansas during the depression. His father found a job as an airplane mechanic, and that's where Brooks learned to fly.

Inside the minds of these two young people were the swirling thoughts of everything that had just happened. They couldn't have known it then, but the two of them would rely heavily on each other if they were going to survive this ordeal. The fates that had brought them together were cruel, but it was possible something good might arise from this.

When darkness came, Ellen helped Brooks through the woods to a small house on the edge of town. The house looked pretty much destroyed. But Ellen explained there was a hidden basement where Brooks could stay. This basement was used by the underground when hiding from the Germans. When they got into the basement, Ellen lit some candles and sliced some bread and cheese for Brooks to eat. After eating Ellen cleaned up Brooks's wounds the best she could and applied a little antiseptic that was stored in the basement. Brooks finally felt a little safer here, and with some food in his stomach, he fell asleep and slept more than 12 hours. Whether it was just luck or divine intervention, Brooks couldn't say for sure, but he truly believed that on Ellen's shoulders were a pair of angel wings. And maybe, just maybe, with her help they could make it out of here alive.

Chapter 15
TIME TO HEAL

When Brooks woke up, Ellen was there. While he had been sleeping she had gone out and met with some of her father's contacts. They got Ellen a little more food and supplies. Brooks thanked Ellen for her care and said, "You saved my life."

She replied, "You saved mine." For the first time since he'd seen her, Ellen gave a little smile. Brooks was certain she was the most beautiful girl he'd ever seen.

That first day while hiding, Brooks and Ellen continued to tell each other things about themselves and how they had gotten to be in this place. Brooks was understandably weak and tired, and his body ached from his various wounds. When darkness fell outside, Brooks was ready to sleep again.

Brooks had been fortunate two nights before when he slept out in the woods. The weather had been unseasonably warm for March in Germany. Now the outside temperature had dropped considerably, and even in the basement Brooks and Ellen could feel the cold. To make matters worse, Brooks started to run a fever. The basement had two sleeping bunks in it, each with one blanket. Ellen gave Brooks a little aspirin that she had, put a cool rag on his head and covered him up with both blankets. Brooks finally drifted off in a fitful sleep. Ellen knew that it was too cold to sleep in the other bunk without a blanket. She also knew that if she slept next to Brooks that they could help to keep each other warm. After Brooks had fallen asleep, Ellen crawled under the covers and placed her back up against his. Immediately she could feel the warmth, and it wasn't long till she fell into the best sleep that she had had in days. During the night, Brooks fever broke. The basement was dark when Brooks woke up. It took a brief moment for Brooks to remember where he was and how he got there. That's when he felt the warm body leaning up against his back. He assumed, and maybe even hoped that it was Ellen. Because all his wounds were on his right side, Brooks was laying on his left side facing the basement wall. He couldn't move his right shoulder much, but ever so carefully, he reached back with his right hand and touched the upper leg of the person sleeping behind him. The touch was enough to cause Ellen to awaken. She too had to remember where she was. In the darkness, you couldn't see it, but Ellen's eyes popped wide open when she remembered she was sleeping next to Brooks. She swung her legs out from under the covers and stood up next to the bunk. She placed her hand on Brooks is back and quietly said, "I'm sorry Brooks. I hope I didn't wake you. I got cold during the night, and I laid down next to you to help you stay warm. I hope you don't mind?"

Brooks was always a little shy around girls, and the thought of the beautiful Ellen sleeping next to him caused him to be a little embarrassed. "No. No.... I don't mind. In fact, it felt really nice having you lying there."

Ellen reached in the darkness and placed her hand on Brooks's forehead. "It feels like you're fever is gone."

"Yah. I think it is. I feel a little better now.... It's just that my body doesn't want to move."

Ellen felt her way to the table and lit a couple of candles. "Can I get you something to eat?"

"Yah. I'm feeling hungry. Can you maybe help me get up from this bunk?"

Ellen tossed the blankets off of his legs and help Brooks swing his legs out and onto the dirt floor. Brooks had to bite his lower lip to keep from crying out from the pain. Ellen helped get him to a chair at the table. Brooks was going to need some time for his wounds to heal. He would rely on Ellen's patience as much as her nursing skills. His recovery would be measured in weeks...not days. Hiding out in the basement meant the routine was pretty much the same for Brooks and Ellen. They ate a little bit, rested a little bit and talked a lot. That evening Ellen helped Brooks back into his bunk and covered him up and blew out the candles. She sat down on the other bunk but kept facing in the direction of Brooks's bunk. Brooks broke the silence, "Uh...Ellen?"

"Yes?"

"I think my fever is coming back…. Could you maybe…lie next to me again to help keep me warm?…. If you don't mind?"

Ellen had a smile on her face as she listened to Brooks phony excuse. "Why no. I don't mind."

Truth was, Ellen didn't mind one bit lying next to this handsome young man who saved her. In her heart she felt like lying next to Brooks might be a habit she could enjoy for the rest of her life. But for now, she kept those thoughts to herself.

The next day was more of the same, but Brooks did tell Ellen he thought he was feeling a little stronger. That night when Ellen helped Brooks in his bunk and blew out the candles, she sat on the other bunk awaiting Brooks's plea. "Uh…Ellen."

"Let me guess," she replied. "You're fever's coming back, and you want me to lie next to you."

"Boy, you really are going to make a great nurse."

Ellen gave a little laugh as she crawled in behind Brooks. After she got settled in, Brooks carefully moved his right hand back and rested it on Ellen's thigh. She reached back and found his hand with hers. As they held hands while lying back to back in the darkness, they each knew the other was wearing a smile.

As the days went on, Brooks continued to heal and started doing a little bit of exercising with his shoulder. The conversations they shared began to get a little more personal, about what each one liked and what some of their dreams were for the future. When they were preparing for bed on the tenth night after Brooks had been shot down, he worked up the nerve to suggest a different sleeping arrangement. Ellen helped him sit down on the edge of the bunk and then Brooks spoke up. "Uh. You know because of my wounds, I always lay on my left side facing the wall. Well, I was just wondering…if you don't mind…if maybe when I lay in that position, maybe I could stay towards the outside edge of the bunk and then you could lay next to the wall, so we could face each other…. If you want to."

Ellen squeezed his hand and said, "Yah Brooks…. I kinda want to."

She crawled in next to the wall and laid her head on Brooks's outstretched left arm.

The nervous Brooks had one more question, "Could I…possibly kiss you?"

Ellen didn't need words to respond. She placed one hand on each side of Brooks's head and pressed her lips to his.

Brooks's first kiss came in a highly unusual time and place. But who really knows when the right time really is. That first kiss was followed by a lot more, and for the moment, these two young people could forget that outside their basement, there was a war going on.

Chapter 16
BAD NEWS

Ten days after Brooks's plane was shot down, a government car arrived in Anomie, Kansas and parked in front of the Trinity Lutheran Church. Early in the morning, there came a knock on the Reverend Foster's door. The Reverend opened the door and saw the two men dressed in military attire. Even before they could speak, Reverend Foster feared he knew what they were going to say. They were there to notify the Borgmans that Brooks had been killed in action, and they would like the Reverend to accompany them to the Borgman house. Reverend Foster hugged his wife Hazel, who was weeping and told the men they will go with them. Reverend Foster took a deep breath and knocked on the Borgman's door. Henry and Ella answered the door together. They saw the strained look on Reverend Foster's face and saw that Hazel had been crying. Then they saw the government car and the two military men. They knew why they were there. Ella fell to the floor weeping. Henry covered his face and leaned against the wall. Reverend Foster said, "Henry, Ella, I'm so sorry."

Minutes passed before they could speak to the military men. The men passed along their condolences. They told Henry and Ella that the Germans had given Brooks's dog tags to the Red Cross. They will be able to tell the Borgmans more at a later date, but they add… "Brooks died a hero." Henry had prayed every night that he would never hear those words. As the military men left, other neighbors and friends came running to the Borgman house as they heard the news. Later that evening Tom Shaw and his wife Debbie were the last to leave. Henry and Ella embraced each other tightly while standing in the kitchen.

Ella said, "I can't believe it's true."

Henry told her, "I have a feeling inside of me that somehow Brooks is still alive."

"But," Ella says, "you heard the men?"

"I know," replied Henry, "but I can't explain this feeling that's inside of me. I know my son, and something is right here in my chest that won't let me believe that he's dead." They turned out the kitchen lights as they went arm in arm into the bedroom.

The news that Brooks had been killed would shake the town of Anomie to its very core. But every single resident knew that the faith in their country and the faith in their God would remain strong. Brooks would not be forgotten.

Chapter 17
THE CREW RETURNS

Another notable thing occurred ten days after that mission. Lieutenant Garbs and the crew of the B-17 bomber arrived back in London. The underground had gotten them aboard a Norwegian freighter headed for England. They were shuttled to the R. A. F. base at High Wycombe where they were warmly greeted by General Aykins and his staff. They were wined and dined for a few days while each of the crew gave a report regarding the bombing of the Ugarde Bridge. Lieutenant Garbs told General Aykins about the actions of Privates Devlin and Dunning and requested that they sit out the remainder of the war in the stockade. General Aykins agreed and notified the military police to bring them in. Every last crew member, as they gave the reports told General Aykins that the mission could not have worked, and they wouldn't be alive if it wasn't for Brooks Borgman. When being told of his exploits, the general marveled at the skill of such a young pilot. He regretfully informed everyone that the Red Cross had been given Brooks's dog tags. He didn't survive. Even though they fully expected that information, it still broke the hearts of each of the crew, when they thought of the effort and sacrifice that this young man had given. A night or two later, after being granted some leave time, Lieutenant Garbs and the guys were at a pub downing some beers when Garbs told the rest of the crew what he planned to do when he got back to America.

"When we get back home, I'm going to go see my family first, but then I am making a trip to Kansas to meet Brooks's mom and dad. I want to tell them firsthand what he did and why I'm alive. Any of you guys are welcome to go with me."

Every single one of the crew said they would go along. All of these men had only known Brooks a few days, but no one would ever be more deeply etched in their memory than the kid from Kansas.

Chapter 18
WILL YOU...?

They would have been surprised to know that the kid from Kansas was trying to build up enough strength to make it home. In the hideout basement, each day Brooks was gaining back some of his energy and mobility. His rib cage no longer hurt unless you hugged him and he could now raise his right arm almost straight out from his body. His right leg was going to take a little while longer as he still couldn't put much weight on it. Ellen continued to take care of him and helped him do exercises to hurry along the healing process. Brooks talked about making an escape from Germany and getting back to the allied lines, but he wasn't sure how to pull that off. One day after eating a small lunch at their table, Brooks got the courage to ask Ellen some questions he'd been pondering for a few days now.

"Ellen. If we could escape from here…what do you want to do?"

"I'm not sure. I guess there's nothing left for me to do in Germany. Maybe if I could get out of the country…I'd go back to my aunt in New York."

"Well. Uh. I was kinda thinking since you said I kinda helped take care of you and you definitely have been taking care of me, well, I was just wondering if maybe you thought that maybe…. Well…. You know…. Like maybe we could take care of each other all the time. Maybe."

Ellen's eyes widened as a slight grin appeared on her face, "Brooks, are you asking me to marry you?"

Brooks nervously looked at the floor as he said, "Well. Yah. I am. Because I thought if you happen to feel the same way towards me as I feel towards you… well…uh…maybe that would be a good idea."

Ellen's grin had turned into a full-blown smile as she replied, "Brooks. Look at me."

Brooks raised his eyes to look into Ellen's.

She said, "Go ahead and ask me."

Brooks had a sheepish smile of his own as he said, "Okay. Ellen. Would you marry me?"

Ellen stood up from her chair and placed her arms around Brooks's neck and kissed him deeply. She continued to hold his head as she backed up just a bit and said, "I think I might be the luckiest girl in the world…. Yes, Brooks, I'd love to marry you."

Brooks let out a huge sigh of relief. They kissed and hugged again and again as the two of them were giddy with the thought of being married. During their days spent here in this basement, Brooks had told Ellen about his parents and the wonderful people of Anomie. He couldn't wait to take her there and let her experience the friendly little town. Ellen was tingling with excitement at all the thoughts that were spinning through her head. Then she looked at Brooks and said, "I hope your parents like me."

Brooks chuckled. "Are you kidding? They're going to love you. Mom always said she wished she had a daughter and I can't think of a better one than you."

Chapter 19
LET'S GO HOME

That night as Brooks and Ellen lay in the bunk, the kisses and the snuggling seemed a bit more special. They didn't bring the subject up that night, but the problem of getting back home was on both of their minds. When they awoke the next morning, Ellen could tell that Brooks was deep in thought. "What are you thinking about Brooks?"

"Oh, I've been thinking for several days now for the best way to try to get home. Were too deep in Germany to walk out...so the only thing that comes to mind is to fly out of here. Ellen, do you know of any German airfields around here?"

"Well Brooks, there used to be an airfield about five miles west of here...but I don't know if it's still there."

Brooks continued, "I think we've got to try to get

there and see if there are still planes there."

"You think we could maybe steal one?"

"Well. I doubt they would loan me one so, yeah, I was hoping to steal one."

"Can you fly a German plane?"

"I think so. We had a little training and basics about German fighter planes, and I can read German, so I should be able to read the instrument panel. I hope."

"Do you think your body is up to the five-mile walk?"

"Well. I guess we'll find out. My ribs and shoulder are good enough, and I'm hoping my leg might loosen up a bit with some walking. We could try to sneak out after dark, and if we go a little ways and I can't take it, we'll come back. Okay?"

Ellen, a little nervous, said, "Okay…. But promise me if you're hurting too bad that will come back and try later."

"I promise. Besides, I want to be real careful to make it back home safely. You see when I get there, there's this special girl that I'm planning to marry."

"Oh really," Ellen replied. "Well, that's funny. If I get back to the states, there's the special guy that I was planning to marry."

Their laughter was followed by a kiss.

Brooks asked, "Do we have any food left that we could take with us?"

"Not really. We're about out of everything."

"Well. We'll take a canteen with some water and after dark tonight will try to head towards that airfield. I hope it's still there."

After dark, they snuck out of the basement that had provided them shelter for almost 3 weeks. Brooks started out using the crutches that Ellen had gotten for him as Ellen walked by his side with a hand on his shoulder to steady him.

Brooks was dealing with some pain, but it was kind of happening as he had hoped, that his leg was indeed loosening up as they traveled. They walked on the road under the cover of darkness being as quiet as they possibly could. They had said that if a vehicle came or they heard something they weren't sure of, they would try to get to the nearby woods. Brooks needed several rest periods along the way. His body just wasn't used to expelling this much energy since he had been wounded. It took them all night, but shortly before dawn, Ellen whispered, "I think the airfield was right over there somewhere. We need to find a place to hide and where you can rest."

Brooks agreed. There was a small grove of timber off to their right, and it looked like a good place to hide. After clearing off the ground a bit, Brooks lay down and quickly went to sleep. Ellen sat next to him and watched as the sky began to brighten with the dawn. When it was light enough, Ellen could make out the gravel road that the Germans used as an airstrip. She let Brooks sleep as she continued to monitor the area for plane activity. She didn't have long to wait. About an hour after the sun came up, Ellen heard airplane engines come to life. She touched Brooks's shoulder and whispered in his ear, "Brooks, there are some planes over there."

Brooks set up so he could see over the brush. He and Ellen watched as two Messerschmitt fighters taxied down the makeshift runway to the north end where they spun around and pointed south. One right behind the other. The planes then paused for a couple of minutes. Brooks told Ellen, "They're letting their engines warm up before they take off."

He was correct and in just a short bit, they headed south and pulled up into the sky. Brooks studied the area and then told Ellen that he thought he had a plan.

Brooks believed these two planes are probably flying support for German ground troops. There's a pretty good chance that these planes do the same thing every day. Brooks pointed to the end of the runway and told Ellen, "You see those weeds down there, right where those planes turned around? Tomorrow morning will hide in those weeds. When those planes turn away from us, I'll jump up on the wing of the back plane and stab the pilot before he closes his cockpit. I'll need you to be right behind me because I'll need help getting his body out of the plane. Then you crawl in behind the seat, and I'll get in and fly the plane."

Ellen asked, "What about the other plane?"

Brooks said, "Since he's in front of us, he won't see us get in the plane. After we take off and get a few miles away from the airfield, I'll shoot him down." Ellen was worried and scared, but she believed in Brooks and agreed to the plan.

But then she told Brooks, "I've never been in a

plane before."

He replied, "Don't worry, you'll be fine." That night Brooks and Ellen huddled together in the brush. They were cold and hungry and a little scared. But mostly they were anxious. Anxious to know if this escape plan could work. The next morning things happened just as Brooks thought they would.

While Brooks and Ellen lay in the weeds, the two fighters turned and parked, just as the day before. Brooks hobbled as fast as he could with Ellen right behind him. He definitely had pain in his leg, but with a major rush of adrenaline and a huge desire to get home, he was able to ignore the pain for the moment. He plopped his butt up on the wing as Ellen helped roll him onto his knees. He drew his knife as he scrambled up the wing and dispatched the German pilot quickly. He tossed the knife away and reached into the cockpit to drag the German out. Ellen was right beside Brooks as she grabbed hold of the pilot's jumpsuit and pulled. The German rolled out of the plane and fell off the wing to the ground. Ellen scrambled as she wedged herself behind the pilot seat. Brooks heard the front plane start to race his engine as he dropped into the cockpit. He and Ellen just got in the plane as the front fighter started to take off. Brooke threw the throttle forward and followed the front plane into the sky. When Brooks felt they were out of hearing of the air-field, he suddenly swung right behind the front plane and fired his machine guns. Brooks's aim was true, and the front plane crumbled and fell to the ground. Steps one and two of their escape plan had succeeded.

Now...could they find their way home? Brooks poured the gas to his plane and headed west hoping he could find the Allied airfield. Brooks let out a little sigh of relief as their plan had worked so far. He yelled over his shoulder at Ellen, "Are you okay?"

She replied, "Yah, I'm fine. But there's not much room in here."

Brooks smiled and nodded in agreement, then focused himself as he watched the sky around them. After flying for a couple of hours, Brooks saw a ground battle taking place below them. From what he could see the Germans had the advantage here as they are advancing on the Allies and the Germans had a tank helping them. Brooks felt it was his duty to try and help the Allied forces. He told Ellen, "I'm going to swing back around and machine-gun that German line. If I get lucky maybe I can knock out that tank."

He swung his German fighter plane around and started an attack run at the ground troops. When the Allied forces saw the German fighter plane, they figured they were in for even more trouble. But before he fired his guns, Brooks changed his position slightly and began strafing the German soldiers. As he neared the tank, Brooks mentally crossed his fingers and released a bomb. That aim that he developed hunting squirrels was true, and the bomb took out the German tank. The American ground troops all cheered as they believed the German pilot had just made a mistake. Brooks flew out and made a U-turn preparing for another run. Again, he machine-gunned the German line, killing some Germans and putting the German offensive in disarray. The Allied troops took advantage of the situation and attacked the Germans. In short order, the stunned German soldiers surrendered. As Brooks flew on west, he dipped his wings back and forth at the Allied lines. Captain Chuck Davis was in charge of the squad of ground troops, and he got on his radio and called the nearest Allied airfield. It happened to be the airfield run by Major Stearns where Brooks had taken off from almost three weeks ago. The captain told Major Stearns that his ground troop was just helped out by a German fighter pilot. The captain believed this pilot may want to defect to the American side. The captain told Major Stearns to watch for this plane, but he may not want to shoot it down. Major Stearns thanked the captain for the information. Major Stearns told two of his new fighter pilots, "Get your planes in the air but don't shoot down the German plane unless he becomes aggressive."

Because of the ground battle that he had just witnessed, Brooks believed he must be over Allied occupied territory. He kept watching for some landmark to indicate where he was. As he and Ellen passed over a little village, he recognized the church in this small town. They flew over this village when he and Lieutenant Garbs went on their flight the second day that Brooks was at the airfield. Brooks told Ellen, "I know where I am! The airfield that I took off from isn't far from here!"

Ellen replied, "That's great! But I was wondering. How will the American planes know not to shoot us down?"

The question hit Brooks like a ton of bricks. Of all the planning that he did, he never thought about getting shot down by his own troops. And just like that Brooks saw two American planes heading his way and he wondered how he could let them know that he wanted to surrender. Brooks yelled at Ellen to look for anything white that he could fly outside of the plane, so the Americans wouldn't shoot them down.

Ellen replied, "I can't find anything white." Brooks was starting to panic when Ellen said, "Here, take this." It was her bra. For a moment Brooks was shocked. The naïve young man can't believe what he's holding in his hand.

"This is your…I can't fly this it's…. How did you..."

Ellen yelled back, "Just forget about it and fly the dang thing! Maybe it will keep us from getting shot down."

He cracked open his cockpit and began flying his "flag" of surrender. The American pilots radioed back to base that the German is flying a flag of surrender, but they didn't tell Major Stearns what they thought the flag actually was. As Brooks tried to keep an eye on the two American planes, he looked ahead and spied the runway of A. F. 29. Brooke slowed down his plane and dropped it down right on the runway. The two American pilots pulled back up into the sky. They would land a few minutes later. Major Stearns wondered what this German pilot was up to and he ordered Bugs to take a machine-gun and a jeep and run down to the end of the runway to pick up this German defector. Bugs was a little nervous as he slid the jeep to a stop twenty yards from the German fighter. Bugs jumped out and readied his machine-gun. Bugs yelled at the pilot descending off the wing to "Get your hands in the air."

Brooks yelled back, "Don't shoot Bugs. It's me."

The puzzled Bugs replied, "Me who?"

With that Brooks turned around and told Bugs, "It's me...Brooks." Bugs threw the machine-gun in the back of the jeep as he sprinted to give Brooks a hug. Bugs was jumping and yelling as Brooks held up his hands and said, "Please don't hug me. It still hurts too bad."

Bugs grabbed hold of each of Brooks's sleeves and yelled in his face. "They said you were dead!"

"Well," Brooks replied, "I just had to play dead for a while till I felt good enough to come back home."

With that, Ellen's voice was heard from the cockpit. "Can I come out now?"

Bugs looked at Brooks, "Who's that?"

Brooks yelled at Ellen to come on out, then he told Bugs, "This is the girl who saved my life." Bug stared as the beautiful Ellen descended from the plane and came over to the jeep. Bugs was still staring when Brooks asked, "Can you take us to the office? I'd like to talk to Major Stearns, and I'm still not walking too well."

Bugs looked back at Brooks, "What did you say?"

Brooks repeated, "Can you drive us to Major Stearns's office?"

The stunned Bugs replied, "Oh yeah, sure. Man is the major going to be surprised!"

Bug slid the jeep to a stop in front of the major's office. He didn't bother helping Brooks or Ellen from the jeep as he ran to the building. Bugs burst into Major Stearns's office. "Major, you ain't gonna believe who was flying that plane." Major Stearns stood up to greet the German pilot. With that Brooks limped into the major's office followed closely by Ellen. Major Stearns plopped back down in his chair in total surprise.

Brooks was wearing a big grin as he saluted the major with his left hand and said, "Private Borgman reporting Sir. Sir, I regretfully report I've lost my plane. But I brought you a different one." Everybody laughed. After some hugging, handshaking and backslapping, Major Stearns asked Brooks what happened. Brooks relayed his story. And when he'd finished, he asked Major Stearns, "What about Lieutenant Garbs? Did they get the bridge and did they make it to Norway?"

Major Stearns told Brooks they destroyed the bridge, made it to Norway and were in England right now waiting to fly home. "Oh my gosh!" said Major Stearns. "Lieutenant Garbs and his crew are leaving for the states tomorrow morning! If we could get you back to England, you could go with them!"

Brooks said, "That would be great, but what about Ellen? Can she come too?"

Major Stearns told Brooks, "From what I know of your story, I think this army would do just about anything you want." The major turned to Bugs and said, "That transport plane is just about to leave to go back to England. Tell him he has two passengers to go with him. And tell him when he gets to England don't tell anyone who he was hauling. I think it would be fun to surprise Lieutenant Garbs and the boys." Major Stearns told Brooks, "Don't worry. While you and Ellen are flying back, I will call General Aykins and get the whole thing approved." Major Stearns continued, "When you get to England, one of the general's staff should pick you up. You'll have to give somebody there a full report of what happened. But you and Ellen should be on that plane tomorrow going home." The major told Brooks and Ellen to get in his jeep, and he drove them to the waiting transport. Major Stearns hopped out of the jeep and escorted Brooks and Ellen to the waiting plane. With his eyes glistening with moisture, Major Stearns told the two, "Most wartime stories are sad ones. I can't tell you how glad I am to have this happy one. Brooks, you're a hero...to me, to Andy and the crew and to everyone back home.... God bless you son."

Chapter 20
THE REUNION

The flight in the transport plane went without incident and Brooks, and Ellen landed in England shortly before dark. One of the general's aides met them on the landing strip and took them by car to the general's headquarters. The general came in and shook Brooks's hand. He said over and over how great it was to have Brooks back. He said, "From the reports, Lieutenant Garbs and his crew gave, son, you are a national hero. Every last man on that crew said they are only alive because of you."

Brooks, slightly embarrassed, replied, "I think they are bragging me up too much. My father always said give anything you do your best effort. That's all I tried to do General, give my best effort."

The general replied, "Son that best effort you gave probably saved more lives than either of us could possibly know." The general called in one of his secretaries. "Brooks, I'm sorry to make you give your report tonight, but we want to get you and Ellen on that plane in the morning."

"It's okay, General," replied Brooks. "I'll do whatever you need me to do."

After giving his report he and Ellen were able to rest for a few hours in the general's quarters. They were awakened and fed a huge breakfast. There was less than a half hour before the plane was scheduled to leave. The general asked if there was anything else he could do. "Well," Brooks asked shyly. "I was kinda thinking about callin' home and telling someone that I'm alive and coming home."

The general said, "That's a good idea, but in America, it's the middle of the night. That kind of call might give your parents a heart attack."

Brooks said, "Yeah, I thought of that. I think I'll call Reverend Foster and let him break the news." The general's secretary made the call and finally got through. It started to ring, and she handed the phone to Brooks. It was the middle of the night when Reverend Foster's phone began to ring.

"Oh, no. This time of the morning is always bad news." He cleared his throat and said, "Hello, Reverend Foster speaking."

From the other end he heard, "Hello Reverend Foster, I know you'll find this hard to believe, but this is Brooks Borgman."

Reverend Foster's eyes popped wide-open, "Who'd you say this was?"

"It's me, Brooks Borgman. I know they said I had been killed, but I was just hiding in Germany until I could escape."

Reverend Foster exclaimed, "Praise the Lord!" Reverend Foster stammered, "But how, did you, I mean what happened? Did you tell your parents?"

Brooks explained that he was aware that it's the middle of the night and he was afraid the shock might be too much for his mom and dad. He told Reverend Foster that he only had a few minutes to talk because the plane bringing him home was about to leave. He asked Reverend Foster that when his parents awoke the next morning could he, please prepare them. Brooks said he would call again when he got back to the states. Then Brooks added, "And ask mom and dad if they could come to Washington D. C. in a couple days. They said they want to give me some kind of award." Reverend Foster said he could do all that, but he had one more question.

"If you're really Brooks, then what memory verse did I give you when you were confirmed?"

Brooks replied, "The 23rd Psalm. The Lord is my shepherd, I shall not want."

Reverend Foster shouted, "Yahoo! Hallelujah and praise the Lord! Brooks Borgman is coming home! Bye son. See you soon." Reverend Foster's wife Hazel was next to him listening to the conversation. Tears of joy streamed down her cheeks as Reverend Foster scooped her up and twirled her around the bedroom all the while shouting, "Praise the Lord."

After hanging up the phone, the general said they

had to hurry. At the airport, Lieutenant Garbs and his crew were already on the plane anxious to take off. One of the crew asked, "What's the holdup?" Lieutenant Garbs said he had talked to the pilot and they were waiting on two more passengers. Probably some big wigs.

The pilot popped his head out of the cockpit and said, "They're here. As soon as they are on board, we'll take off."

The first person to come through the door was General Aykins. Lieutenant Garbs and his crew jumped to attention. "Excuse me, General," said Lieutenant Garbs, "I wasn't aware you were on this flight."

The general smiled and said, "At ease. I'm not on this flight. I just came here to introduce to you your other two passengers." Ellen came through the door and catcalls rang out. The general motioned for them to be quiet. He continued, "This young lady's name is Ellen and she is traveling in the company of her fiancé. I think maybe you know this guy. Gentlemen, say hello again to Brooks Borgman!" Brooks stepped in. Total silence fell in the plane. Several of the men made the sign of the cross.

Someone said, "It's a ghost. You're dead. I saw your plane crash."

The general said, "I assure you guys he's very much alive. And on this trip home, he's got a great story to tell you." The general continued, "The Allied forces owe each and every one of you a huge debt that we can never totally repay. I want you folks to have a good flight home. After I'm off the plane, if you look under this tarp up front, you'll find a case of champagne. Hopefully, I'll see you boys back in the states in not too long. I salute every one of you." The general left. Lieutenant Garbs and his crew rushed to the front of the plane to hug Brooks. Backslapping, shouting and tears were mixed together as these men try to comprehend someone standing there that they were sure was dead.

The pilot yelled, "If you guys will take a seat, we'll be on our way."

Chapter 21

GREAT NEWS!

The flight home was one big celebration. Brooks told everyone his story, including how Ellen and he had helped each other and then fell in love. He told them about the time spent in the basement, about the healing and the exercise and about the stealing of the German fighter plane they used to get back to Allied lines. He did not tell them what he used as his flag of surrender. Then Brooks asked, "What about you guys? How did you get back?"

Lieutenant Garbs replied, "Our story not nearly as exciting as yours. The Ruby Sinclair got us to Norway. We were found by the underground, and they got us civilian clothes and got us on a freighter going back to England. We spent a few days in London and… well…here we are." The champagne was done by the time they neared New York. Lieutenant Garbs told

Brooks, "I only saw you fly one day. But for my money, you're the best damn pilot I ever saw. When I found out your real name was Brooklyn, I thought that was a bit strange." He cleared his throat, then continued, "But I'm vowing to you this day. If the good Lord ever blesses me with a son, I'm going to name him Brooklyn, and I want you to be his godfather." A cheer went up on the plane, and all the rest of the guys said the same thing.

The plane landed in New York, and all on board were taken to a hotel where they would be allowed to enjoy the day in the Big Apple.

Brooks desperately wanted to call his mom and dad, but since he was in New York, he thought he should call his godfather, Andrew first. With help from the operator, Brooks got his phone call through to Andrew's place of work. When someone answered the phone, Brooks asked, "Could I please speak to Andrew Borgman?"

The person on the other end replied, "Well. He's kinda busy right now. Can I give him a message?"

Brooks said, "This is very important. Could I please talk to him?"

Brooks could hear the guy on the other end of the phone yell across the room. "Hey, Andrew. Somebody wants to talk to you. They said it was important."

When Andrew got on the phone, he sounded a bit annoyed as he said, "Yah. Who is this?"

"Andrew. You may not believe this, but this is Brooks."

Andrew had received Ella's letter telling him that

Brooks had been killed in action. And now there was somebody claiming to be Brooks. Was this some kind of joke? But his voice sounded like Brooks. Andrew's mind continued to race as he tried to think of something to say.

Brooks broke the silence, and he continued, "I'm sure you heard that I had been killed. But actually I was just wounded, and I've been hiding out in Germany till I could make my escape. I've just arrived in New York, and I was hoping I could see you."

Andrew was still in shock as he asked, "So this is really Brooks?"

"Yes."

"And you're not dead?"

"No."

"And you're in New York?"

"Yes."

Brooks could hear Andrew scream at the top of his lungs. He then yelled to his coworkers, "My godson is alive! Brooks is alive!"

Andrew came back on the phone, "So where are you at?"

"We are at the Plaza Hotel."

"Okay. I'll be there in an hour. Don't go anywhere!"

"I won't. See you then Andrew."

Brooks had told Ellen about Andrew, and now he felt good that she soon would be meeting him.

Now Brooks could make the phone call that he wished he could have made for more than the last three weeks.

Back in Kansas after Reverend Foster had got the

call from Brooks, both the Reverend and his wife began contacting all of their church family telling them the fantastic news. Almost the whole congregation met at the church shortly after daybreak. They brought coffee and punch, cookies, donuts, biscuits, rolls and such. Then they all walked to the north end of town where the Borgmans lived. Henry and Ella had just awakened. Ella was going to prepare coffee. Henry sat down at the table and stared out the window. They had done little talking since they got the news. Henry and Ella heard the noise at the same time. They looked at each other, the sound they heard was singing. They went out their kitchen door and onto the porch. They were puzzled as Reverend Foster led the congregation up to Henry and Ella's house. Reverend Foster could barely contain himself.

He began, "Henry, Ella, I want you to sit down right here on the porch." Henry and Ella sat down. Reverend Foster continued, "Henry, Ella, the Lord indeed works in mysterious ways. A few hours ago, I got a phone call.... It was Brooks. He's alive!" Ella burst into tears as Hazel embraced her to keep her from falling over. "I know this is hard to believe, but he's alive, and he's on his way home right now!" Tears welled up in Henry's eyes, but he continued to stare in stunned silence. Reverend Foster said, "I talked to him. He's coming home. He's going to call you later when they get back in the states. He didn't want to shock you, that's why he called me." Reverend Foster grabbed the shoulders of Henry and said, "Henry! Did you hear what I said? Brooks is alive."

Tears flowed down Henry's cheeks as he replied softly, "I know. I've always known." With that, the gathering turned into a celebration. They all partook of the food and drink provided, and all the congregation took turns hugging Henry and Ella on this wonderful news. Gradually most of the town folks went back home, but Reverend Foster, Hazel, Tom Shaw and Debbie stayed with Henry and Ella. Finally, the Borgman's phone rang. Henry and Ella were hesitant to answer it. Reverend Foster picked up the phone. It was Brooks.

Reverend Foster was grinning from ear to ear as he told Brooks, "Why yes they're right here." He handed the phone to Henry. Henry put the phone to his ear, but no words would come.

Brooks said, "Dad, I'm so sorry I put you through this but I had to play dead so I could hide."

Henry spoke, "It's okay son. When can we see you?"

Brooks replied, "The day after tomorrow. They're gonna give me some kind of medal in Washington D.C. They want you and mom to be there. Do you think you can catch a train to Washington D. C.?"

Henry replied, "Brooks, we'll be there if we have to walk."

Brooks said, "Dad, I have to get off the phone. Tell mom that I love you both and I will see you in two days."

Henry said, "We love you too son."

Henry reached out and embraced Ella. Together they cried their tears of joy. The Fosters and the Shaws slipped out of the house and left the Borgmans with their thoughts.

Back in New York, after Brooks had called his dad, it was Ellen's turn to pass on good news. She called her Aunt Caroline to tell her she was safe and back in New York. Her aunt was delighted to hear that she was in America and that she had a fiancé. Then Ellen had to pass on the bad news that her parents were both victims of the war. This saddened her aunt greatly, but Aunt Caroline told Ellen if there was anything she could do for her, just let her know. As Ellen hung up the phone, there was a knock on their hotel room door. They heard Andrew yell, "How's my favorite godson!"

Chapter 22
THE HERO

The train the Borgmans needed to catch left Jukes-ville at 7:00 a.m. the next morning. Reverend Foster and Hazel drove Henry and Ella to the station. Henry was worried about how much the tickets would cost because he hadn't been working the past several weeks and they didn't have much cash. When they walked up to the ticket booth there stood Tom Shaw. He had purchased two first-class tickets for Henry and Ella to Washington D. C.

Henry was all choked up, and he told Tom, "I'll pay you back."

Tom replied, "Henry, what you and Ella and Brooks have meant to this town and to me personally, I could never repay with one thousand tickets." He hugged Henry. "Go bring your son home." As Henry and Ella started walking to their train car, Tom added,

"And you tell that boy of yours I'm going to take a hickory switch to his backside for taking ten years off my life." Henry and Ella laughed and waved and got on the train.

Back in New York, Brooks and Ellen enjoyed the afternoon and evening with Andrew. They went out to eat and spent their time reminiscing.

The next morning, Brooks, Ellen, Lieutenant Garbs and all the crew were transported to Washington D. C. As the time for the ceremony drew near, Brooks kept watching the crowd, looking for his mom and dad. The officials had seated Ellen in the front row and left two seats for Henry and Ella. Some of the other guys were already being recognized for their accomplishments when Brooks saw them. His mom and dad were being escorted to the front row next to Ellen. Then it dawned on Brooks. He had never told his mom and dad about Ellen. He thought, well, maybe they won't talk, and after the ceremonies, I can introduce them and explain to mom and dad the whole thing.

Brooks was the last man recognized. While they were waiting, Ellen, who was sure that the people next to her were Brooks's mom and dad, turned to Henry and Ella and asked, "Is Brooks your son?" Henry and Ella proudly smiled and replied that, yes he was. Ellen held out her hand and introduced herself. She said, "Brooks and I helped each other while we were hiding from the Germans."

Ella hugged Ellen and said, "Oh thank you. Whatever you did to bring our son back to us, we can't possibly repay you."

For twenty seconds they sat in silence, then Ellen turned to Ella and said, "Brooks asked me to marry him!"

Ella's jaw dropped. Henry's eyes popped wide open. Ellen continued, "I'm sorry to shock you like that if you want me to leave I'll go." Ella didn't know what to say. Suddenly Henry broke out in a huge smile. He reached across and gave Ellen a big hug and a kiss on the cheek.

Henry told Ellen and Ella, "You know that's one thing that us Borgman men all have in common. We always pick the most beautiful girls to be our wives." Ellen had tears running down her cheeks as she hugged Ella.

Ella smiled and said, "I don't believe it. I finally have a daughter!" Ella and Ellen hugged again.

Then they heard the P. A. Announcer say, "And here to present the Congressional Medal of Honor for gallantry above and beyond the call of duty is President Harry S. Truman. This country's highest honor is now bestowed on Brooklyn Borgman."

There were handshakes to be given and pictures to be taken, and finally, Brooks could get away. He rushed to his mom and dad hugging and kissing them. Then he stepped back and said, "Mom and dad. I'm sorry I didn't tell you sooner. This young lady's name is Ellen."

Before Brooks could continue, Ella broke in, "Oh Brooks we've already met. I am so excited to have a daughter. I have a feeling that she is someone very special." Brooks let out a sigh of relief. With that, Henry, Ella, Brooks and Ellen all began talking at the same time. Each one has so much to say, and it seemed there was not enough time to say everything they wanted to. Henry and Ella desperately wanted to know all that had happened to Brooks, and they fired off questions faster than Brooks could answer. Brooks was more interested in relaying to them all the things Ellen did for him and how incredibly important she had become in his life. They were so engrossed in conversation that they failed to notice the group of people approaching them.

Suddenly Brooks felt a hand on his shoulder, and he turned to see the smiling face of Lieutenant Andy Garbs. Right behind Andy was the rest of the Ruby Sinclair crew along with all of their family members that had come for the ceremonies. Brooks and Andy embraced as the rest of the crew swatted him on the back amid shouts of "Way to go kid."

Brooks 'eyes glistened as he turned back to his parents and said, "Mom, Dad, these are the guys from the B-17 that I flew along with. They're the greatest bomber crew in all America as far as I'm concerned." He continued, "Lieutenant Garbs, guys, these are my parents, Henry and Ella Borgman and well you already know Ellen."

Everyone in the group shouted "Hi" and "Hello," as Lieutenant Garbs shook the hand of both Ella and Henry.

Andy then continued, "Mister and Mrs. Borgman. I'm speaking on behalf of my whole crew and our families. We would not be here if it wasn't for your son. In the short time we got to know each other, he proved to be the most skilled fighter pilot any of us ever saw. I realize that you can learn that stuff through training, but it wasn't only the skills that set your son apart. Brooks has inside him the heart and desire to always do his best and to give everything he's got to help those around him. That's not something that he learned in basic training. That's something that was instilled inside him by his parents. You have every right to be proud of the medal that he wears on his chest. But you should be even more proud of what's inside the chest that this medal adorns. Thank you for sharing your son with us."

Henry's eyes were moist, and the lump in his throat wouldn't allow any words to flow. Ella used a tissue to dab at the tears on her cheeks.

Lieutenant Garbs put out his arm and embraced a young lady who was standing next to him. She was obviously his girlfriend or fiancé. He then spoke again, "I told the other guys on my plane that if the good Lord ever blesses me with a son, I'm going to name him Brooklyn. And I would like your son to be his godfather."

Ella stepped forward and threw her arms around Lieutenant Garbs. Henry re-shook his hand, and the thank-yous are many. The family members made their way up to shake Brooks's hand or plant a kiss on his cheek. Several more minutes passed before the group realized they are among the last people to remain in the ceremony area. Goodbyes were exchanged, and everyone told one another, "Don't forget to write."

When Brooks, Ellen, Henry and Ella arrived out on the sidewalk, Henry announced, "Brooks I just thought of the fact that we don't have any arrangements for a place to stay. I mean, can you go home now or what exactly is your timetable?"

Brooks smiled, "Well dad, it's my understanding that we have rooms reserved for all of us in that fancy hotel just down the street. I talked to a Colonel Beglin backstage, and he said we should check in there. He said that the rooms and all our meals are being paid for by the two senators from Kansas. As far as my schedule goes, I'm not really sure. Everything has happened so fast. Colonel Beglin said he would be in touch with me in the morning."

Brooks picked up his mom and dad's suitcase, and the four started their short walk to the hotel. For the moment the talking had subsided. Brooks hardly noticed the weight of the suitcase. The limp in his leg was all but gone. Perhaps he stood a little more erect. His shoulders seemed a bit broader. Maybe his chest stuck out a little bit more. The world will forever see him as a hero. Brooks Borgman sees himself as Henry and Ella's son and Ellen's fiancé. What more could a man want?

Chapter 23
WELCOME HOME

The next morning Henry, Ella, Brooks, and Ellen were eating breakfast in the hotel dining room when Colonel Beglin came up to their table. Brooks stood to attention and Henry also stood up to greet the Colonel. Colonel Beglin shook Henry's hand and said, "Please, please be seated. Sorry to interrupt your meal. I don't suppose I have to tell you, you have a special son and fiancé."

Henry and Ella replied, "Thank you," at the same time. Henry added, "We are very proud of Brooks."

"As you should be," said Colonel Beglin. "I was wondering if you folks could hang around Washington D. C. a couple more days?"

"I suppose we can," answered Henry. "But can you tell us when Brooks can come home with us?"

"Certainly, certainly," came the Colonel's reply.

"The way this works is, we need a couple of days to get Brooks's discharge papers together, and at the same time, we are putting together the paperwork for Ellen to stay here forever. I'm assigning one of my aides to be stationed right outside the hotel, and he'll be happy to give you guys a tour of the city. Anything you want to see. Courtesy of the Army. Also, we are making arrangements for your train ride back home. You should be arriving back in Kansas around noon on Saturday. Would that be all right?"

Everyone agreed that would be great.

Before leaving Colonel Beglin said, "Brooks, Ellen, I'll have a few papers for you guys to sign. I'll bring them here to the hotel tomorrow evening."

"Thank you sir."

Before heading out on the sightseeing tour, Henry called Reverend Foster to tell him of their planned time to arrive home. Henry and Ella knew the town was wanting to have a welcome home celebration and he hoped this would give them enough time to get the word out.

For the next day and a half, the foursome saw the sights of the nation's capital. The White House, the Pentagon, the monuments, Arlington Cemetery and more. But for Henry, Ella and Brooks, the anxiousness to get back home was growing. Ellen was also anxious to see her future new hometown, but she also harbored a few fears of all the things that lay in front of her. One thing that helped ease those fears was how loved Henry and Ella made her feel. They reminded her of her own parents.

They signed all the necessary papers that evening and the next morning found them boarding the train that would take them to Kansas City. After switching trains there, they would start the final leg of their journey for Jukesville.

Back in Kansas, celebration preparations were underway. There would be parties in both Jukesville and Anomie. The high school band was rehearsing. Banners were being hung over the streets in both towns. Lots of baking going on and the men of Trinity Lutheran Church were planning on barbecuing several hogs. Reverend Foster was the appointed master of ceremonies, and he was busy seeing to it that all things were ready. And that his welcome speech was written.

Henry and Ella never told Brooks that there would be a welcome home party, but Brooks kind of expected the town or the church would do something. He didn't feel like he did anything more than the rest of his comrades would do, but he'd have to admit that seeing his friends and neighbors again would be really special.

It was early Saturday morning when the group switched trains in Kansas City. Everything was fairly quiet as the Borgmans took their seats. Then the conductor came by to check their tickets. He looked at Brooks a few seconds, then said, "Hey. You're that Borgman fellow. That pilot that I read about in the paper."

Brooks smiled sheepishly and nodded, "Yah. That's me."

He reached out to shake Brooks's hand, "Welcome

home son. We sure do appreciate everything you've done."

"Thank you. I was just trying to do my job."

"From what I've read, you've done more than just your job. You made everybody in America real proud. Especially us folks here in Kansas."

Brooks just smiled and nodded again.

There weren't many passengers on that early morning train. But a mother traveling with her two teenage daughters heard the conductor's conversation with Brooks. When the conductor stepped aside, the three women approached the Borgmans. The mother introduced herself then said, "I don't mean to interrupt you, but I heard the conductor say who you were. Thank you so much, young man."

Again Brooks smiled and replied, "Thank you for the kind words. And you're welcome."

The mom continued, "If it's not too much bother, could I get a picture of you with my daughters?"

Brooks looked first at Ellen, then his parents. They were all smiling. Ellen gave him a push and said, "Well go on. The ladies are waiting for you."

Brooks stood up in the aisle with one daughter on each side. As the mother readied her camera, she asked, "Can you put an arm around each girl?"

Ellen covered her mouth so as not to giggle out loud. This big strong hero of a future husband was more nervous getting his picture taken with these two young ladies then he was in the cockpit of the fighter plane.

The mother got the picture she wanted and thanked Brooks again. Then everyone returned to their seats.

Ellen could hardly keep from laughing as she kept her face turned towards the window. Then she spoke, "Well. I guess I should be jealous of the way you're going around and hugging every woman you see."

Brooks's eyes got big as he defended himself. "Now wait a minute honey, they asked me to do that. I…" Ellen broke out in laughter as she turned and hugged her special man. Henry and Ella were laughing also at the shyness of their son that they loved so much.

Henry put his hand on Brooks's shoulder. "You'd better get used to pictures, hugs and kisses, son. I'd say before the days over, you're gonna get a lot of them."

As the train rolled along toward the Jukesville station, the Borgmans kept watching out the windows. Whenever they spied a landmark of some kind, they would point it out to Ellen.

The conductor came down the aisle and looked at the Borgmans. "We'll be in Jukesville in ten minutes."

Everyone was anxious to get home, but Brooks's mind was full of thought. In ten more minutes, he would have completed a circle that was longer and more dangerous than he could possibly have imagined. His guardian angel was sure on duty. Not only did he help protect him, but in the process, he found a soulmate who would be by his side for the rest of his life. Brooks was happy.

The passenger cars clanked together as the train started to slow down for the Jukesville station. The Borgmans pressed their faces against the window as they tried to see if anyone was there waiting. As they passed the last view-blocking building, they all gasped. "Oh my goodness," exclaimed Ella. It was not anyone. It was more like everyone. People were standing side-by-side all around the station. The street to the west of the station was lined with police cars and fire trucks. Henry was in awe. "I think half the state of Kansas is here!"

The folks that were gathered there didn't know which train car the Borgmans were in, but it really didn't matter. They were yelling and waving at the whole train. The conductor was smiling from ear to ear as he escorted the Borgmans to the exit. "I'll take care of your bags." He pointed toward the crowd. "I think these fine folks are waiting for you."

Henry was beaming as he told his son, "Brooks. You go first." When Brooks appeared in the doorway, a cheer arose that was almost deafening. Brooks's mind was reeling. "I couldn't possibly know this many people. What are they all doing here?"

With his hand on Brooks's shoulder, Henry shouted, "You may not know all of them. But they know who you are. They just want you to know they appreciate what you've done."

Brooks's smile grew in intensity as he tried to wave at people in every direction.

"Welcome home son!"

Brooks looked in the direction from which those words had come. It was Reverend Foster. Brooks stepped toward the Reverend and stuck out his hand. Reverend Foster stepped right past Brooks's outstretched hand and wrapped him in a bear hug. And just like that, Reverend Foster's wife Hazel was in on the hug, and they were quickly joined by Tom and Debbie Shaw. Still, in awe, Brooks asked Reverend Foster, "Who are all these people?"

"These are all folks from around the area that just want to let you know how grateful they are for all you've done."

"I don't think I deserve all of this."

"Well, you just let us be the judge of that. In the meantime, just have fun Brooks. This day is for you."

Reverend Foster escorted Brooks and his family to the west end of the station platform. There was a microphone waiting there and next to the microphone was the principal from Jukesville High School, John Baker. After shaking Brooks's hand, Mister Baker motioned to the crowd for a little quiet. He then spoke. "Welcome home Brooks." A roar went up from the crowd. He continued, "I can't tell you how wonderful it is to have you back home. Our towns, our state and these United States all want you to know how proud we are of you." Another roar arose from the people gathered. The principal went on, "Brooks, the main part of today's celebration will take place in your hometown of Anomie. We'll be having a parade of sorts as you motor there, but before we go, is there anything you would like to say to this crowd?"

Brooks took a deep breath and edged up to the mic. "Well, I guess I really don't know what to say. I'm really, really surprised. I want to thank each and every one of you for being here. It seems like a lot of folks have gone out of their way to plan this big party. I really appreciate this. I don't know what else to say. I guess...uh… Let's get the parade started."

The crowd applauded and yelled some more, and then folks made their way to their awaiting vehicles. Some of the people here in Jukesville weren't planning on going to the celebration in Anomie, but a high percentage of the crowd was going. Reverend Foster led Brooks and his family to the lead police car. It was Anomie's only police car, and it was driven by Sheriff Douglas. He shook Brooks's hand and told Brooks to ride in the front seat with him. Henry, Ella and Ellen sat in the backseat. Before getting in the car, Henry asked Tom Shaw, "What about our luggage?"

Tom smiled and replied, "Don't worry about it. We've got people taking care of that. Just go have fun."

Sheriff Douglas eased his squad car onto the street, then kicked on his flashing lights and siren. Right behind Anomie's police car was one from Jukesville. Then came Anomie's two fire trucks and two more from Jukesville. Cars filled in behind them as they headed for Anomie. It seemed that every crossroad or driveway they passed had people waiting there with signs that read "Welcome Home" or "We are proud of you." Brooks smiled and waved, but his humble nature just wouldn't let him believe he deserved all this.

As they rolled into Anomie, a huge banner was hung over the street that read, "Welcome Home Brooks." Sheriff Douglas pulled up and parked just to the east of the Trinity Lutheran Church. Brooks's jaw dropped when he saw all the tents, picnic tables and chairs sitting on the church grounds. On the tables set up next to the church, there seemed to be enough food to feed the whole state of Kansas. Brooks stepped out of the car and was quickly joined by Henry, Ella and Ellen. Brooks swiveled his head as he took in the whole picture, then simply said, "Wow!"

With that, he realized he was neglecting Ellen. He grabbed her hand and said, "This is my home. Welcome to Anomie."

Ellen hugged him and replied, "Oh Brooks. It's just like you described it, only better. It's so beautiful. And these people are so friendly. I love it already."

The people coming from the cars gathered with those already on the church grounds and in a few short moments the place was crowded. Reverend Foster found the Borgmans and ushered them to the makeshift platform set up by the church. On the platform were four chairs and Reverend Foster told the Borgmans to have a seat. With that, he stepped up to the microphone that had been set up for this occasion.

"If I could have everyone's attention please. Please, folks, a little quiet so we can get on with the festivities. I know that the reason you are all here is to shake the hand of this young man and thank him for all he has done, so I'll keep my part short. I'll bet you never heard that from a preacher before have you? Before I pass along a few of my thoughts, I'd like to say a little prayer. Would you bow your heads? Heavenly Father. Thank you for once again reminding us that all things are possible with you. Your guardian angel saw fit to return this young man here today. He left this town to serve his country, and he returns to us as a hero. There are no words to fully show you our appreciation, so we hope our heartfelt thank-yous will be sufficient. We know, dear Lord, that many of this country's soldiers will not be coming home. Be with those families, and we pray that your peace be laid upon them. Join with us now, Heavenly Father, in this time of celebration. To thee be all the glory. Amen."

"Folks, we are so glad that you have come here today to help us celebrate this special event. There will be food and drink available all afternoon. I know many of you want to talk to Brooks and that's fine but please not all at once. Give him a little room. I'm going to let Brooks have the mic here in a moment, but first I've got a little bit to add. Brooks, I'm reminded of the story of the prodigal son. Don't get me wrong, you're nothing like the prodigal son. But there are a couple of lines at the end of that parable that fit here. Bring hither the fatted calf and kill it and let us eat and be merry. For this my son was dead and is alive again; he was lost and is found. God has blessed you, Brooks. And he's blessed all of us as well. After we got the news and the Army said you were dead, I had several long talks with your mom and dad. And every time when our talks broke up, your dad told me the same thing. He said he felt you were still alive. He said he could feel you in his heart.… Henry was right. Now your parents see their son return. But you are also a son of this community and of this state and of this country. I predict the Lord has big plans for you and your future family. But before I go any further, I'll let you introduce your fiancé. Welcome home, my son. Welcome home."

The crowd all cheered as Reverend Foster hugged

Brooks, Ellen, Henry and Ella. He then motioned for Brooks to take the mic. As he approached the mic the roar of the crowd got even louder. When the noise died down Brooks began, "Well. I'm not very good at making speeches. When Reverend Foster said there might be big plans in my future, I hope he wasn't figuring on me becoming a preacher because I doubt I could do that."

The crowd laughed.

"I guess first I should introduce my family. This is my dad Henry and my mom Ella. And this is my fiancé Ellen Miden. I wouldn't be here if Ellen hadn't nursed me back to life. I guess she could see that I was someone who needed a lot of help, so she agreed to marry me."

More laughter from the people. Brooks was quiet for a moment as he thought about the words he wanted to say. "Since I've been back in the United States, several people have used the word hero when talking about me. I don't look at myself that way. I was a part of a group of people that were asked to do a job. A hard and terrible job. Before I left, dad told me to do my best and try to protect the people around me. I did the best I could. And I think I have a lot of you to thank. Of course my family, but all of you in this town and the surrounding area have always made me feel safe and protected. I guess I was just trying to give a little bit of that feeling back somehow to the guys I was with over there. I know I have all of you to thank. And I know I can never actually repay you. But I'm going to try to be a good neighbor to every one of you. And

I hope to call Anomie home for the rest of my life.... Thank you, everybody."

The crowd erupted with more cheers and applause. Brooks waved at the people then turned away to hide the tears on his cheeks. Henry, Ella and Ellen all rose out of their chairs and joined in a group hug in the middle of the platform. Reverend Foster walked up to the Borgmans and patted Brooks on the back and then stepped back up to the microphone. "Folks... I'm reminded of another passage that says, 'greater love hath no man than this, that a man lay down his life for his friends.' We are all incredibly grateful that Brooks's life was spared. But the good Lord knows... that he would have done it if he would have had to. Well, that tells me that God isn't done with Brooks yet. I think it's fantastic that whatever that future might be, it's going to happen right here in Kansas."

The crowd applauded some more, and then Reverend Foster continued, "Folks, I think I've said enough. Let's get the celebration going. Brooks and his family will be mingling through the crowd. Please say hi if you can. There's plenty of refreshments, so all of you have a good time."

With that, the welcome home party got underway. For the next two hours, Brooks shook more hands and had his picture taken more times than he could remember. Ellen was by his side almost all the time except when Ella was introducing her to a number of the town folks. When Brooks and Ellen finally had a couple of free minutes, they each grabbed a pork sandwich and a glass of lemonade. They tasted great. Just as he finished his sandwich, he felt a hand rest on his shoulder. When he turned, he was staring into the smiling face of Gene Telford. Brooks bear hugged this man who meant so much to him. When words finally came to him, Brooks said, "I was hoping you'd be here."

"Are you kidding!" replied Gene. "Wild horses couldn't keep me away." Gene looked Brooks up and down. "You're looking good kid."

"Thanks. Oh, I was hoping I'd see you! I have something for you." Brooks reached in his shirt pocket and pulled out the World War I medallion that Gene had loaned him when he left for basic training. "Here. I told you I'd bring it back."

Gene was too choked up to say anything. He smiled and nodded. He then cleared his throat and said, "Thanks. But you know, I've been thinking about it. I want you to keep it."

"But Gene. It's yours. And you're right. It brought me good luck."

"Well, I'm glad for that. I know that little insignia doesn't mean as much is that hardware you're wearing on your chest, but...I'd consider it a personal favor if you keep that thing too. Brooks, I don't have any sons and no grandkids. So maybe you can give it to one of your kids someday. Maybe it'll bring them good luck too."

Brooks stared down at the little insignia he was holding. Brooks nodded and with a broken voice replied, "Yah. I'm sure it will."

"Well," said Gene, "I'd better let you talk to the others. I'll see you in church tomorrow."

Brooks looked up and smiled, "Yah.... Yah you will."

Gene turned and walked away. Ellen had been standing alongside Brooks and entered the conversation. She placed her hand on Brooks and asked, "You okay?"

"Yah.... I'm fine." He leaned over and kissed Ellen. Then he broke into a big smile. He asked her, "Did you hear what Gene said?"

Ellen was a little puzzled. "Yah. I heard what you guys said to each other."

"He said we're going to have kids."

Ellen broke into a big smile too. She gave Brooks a coy little look and replied, "Well, I certainly hope so."

Evening time was starting to approach and slowly the crowd was diminishing. Brooks and Ellen had a little time to themselves, and they walked to the east edge of the church lot. Standing in the lengthening shade of the big trees they relished the opportunity to just hold each other.

Ellen said, "We'd better go back to the church."

Brooks answered, "Yah. I suppose so. It's really nice just being in the peace and quiet."

Ellen looked and saw Ella helping Hazel Foster and other ladies beginning to pack up some leftover food. She gave Brooks a kiss. "I'm going to go help your mom."

She began walking when Brooks replied, "She's your mom too."

Ellen glanced back and gave Brooks a smile then continued on to help the ladies.

All was quiet around Brooks, and suddenly he sensed he wasn't alone. He looked to his right and saw the shadow of a man coming through the trees. He got into the illumination of the fading light. It was Henry. His dad spoke, "Kind of a busy day. Wasn't it?"

"Yah. I'm overwhelmed."

"Our family is really lucky to live in a town like this. The people really care for one another."

All was quiet for a few moments. Then Brooks said, "Dad, I'm really sorry I put you through this."

"Don't worry about it son. Everything came out all right."

Brooks continued, "Reverend Foster said you knew I wasn't dead. How'd you know?"

"I'm not sure. I just felt it in my heart. Somehow I felt sure that the bridge between you and me wasn't broken. I knew we'd meet again. I just knew it."

When you're weary, feeling small

"I love you dad."

When tears are in your eyes,
I'll dry them all, I'm on your side

"I love you son."

Oh, when times get rough,
and friends just can't be found

Like a bridge over troubled water,
I will lay me down

Like a bridge over troubled water,
I will lay me down

Father and son shared a long passionate hug. When their bodies separated, they kept their arms clasped to one another. If a passerby would have looked that way they might have supposed that the silhouette of these two men resembled the superstructure of a bridge. But the passerby couldn't have possibly fathomed the strength that held the silhouette together. Steel and mortar can erode with time. But the love between a father and son never weakens. It's the strongest bond known to man.

Is even stronger than…Brooklyn's Bridge.

The End

When you're down and out
When you're on the street
When evening falls so hard
I will comfort you
I'll take your part, oh, when darkness comes
And pain is all around
Like a bridge over troubled water
I will lay me down
Like a bridge over troubled water
I will lay me down

(Song lyrics: Bridge Over Troubled Water by Simon & Garfunkel)

ALSO BY GARY GUEST

Gary is the author of the bestselling Fertilizer for the Funnybone series which is available on Amazon and Barnes & Noble

YOU MAY FOLLOW GARY ON FACEBOOK AND GARYGUEST.NET